the LIGHT PRINCESS

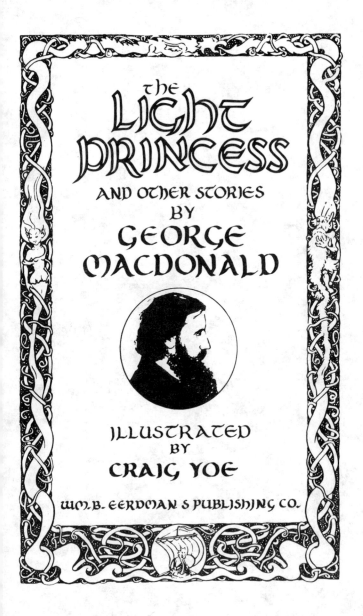

The LIGHT PRINCESS

AND OTHER STORIES

BY

GEORGE MACDONALD

ILLUSTRATED BY

CRAIG YOE

WM. B. EERDMANS PUBLISHING CO.

CONTENTS

ILLUSTRATIONS

The story-title decoration is based on an anagram George
MacDonald invented from the letters of his name. It was adopted
as a family emblem.

PUBLISHER'S NOTE

"IT must be more than thirty years ago that I bought . . . *Phantastes*. A few hours later I knew I had crossed a great frontier. . . . What it actually did to me was to convert, even to baptise, my imagination."

In those words C. S. Lewis, creator of the Narnia Chronicles, reported his discovery of George MacDonald, one of the nineteenth-century innovators of modern fantasy. Thanks in part to Lewis's appreciation—"I regarded him as my master"—MacDonald came to influence not only Lewis himself but that circle of Lewis's friends in Oxford who called themselves the Inklings. Included were Charles Williams and—more famously—J. R. R. Tolkien, who has paid his own tribute to the "power and beauty" of MacDonald's accomplishment.

George MacDonald was born in 1824, five years later than Queen Victoria; he died four years after her, in 1905. His birthplace was Huntly, Aberdeenshire, in Northwest Scotland, and his Scottish background shows through his work, in its kindly but unsentimental astringency and its love of the commonplace, even more clearly than does the Victorian world in which he later moved as a resident of London. In 1840 he entered Kings College at Aberdeen, and ten years later he became clergyman to a chapel at Arundel, a position he left in 1853 to begin what was to be a long career as highly respected writer, lecturer, and preacher. Among his literary friends were Carlyle, Tennyson, William Morris, and Lewis Carroll. In 1872 he travelled on a spectacularly successful lecture tour of the United States, where he was hailed by the popular press and saw such prominent men of letters as Whittier and Emerson.

MacDonald wrote a number of conventional Victorian novels, modestly successful in his own time but of interest now largely as period pieces. It is for his entrancing fantasy that MacDonald is justly revered today by an enthusiastic and growing readership. These fantasy works include the adult "Faerie Romances" *Phantastes* and *Lilith* and three full-length children's classics: *At the Back of the North Wind, The Princess and the Goblin*, and *The Princess and Curdie*.

Much of MacDonald's best fantasy writing, however, is found in his shorter stories, which in his lifetime were published in such collections as *Adela Cathcart* (1864) and *The Gifts of the Child Christ, and Other Tales* (1882). In the present volume and its companion volumes in THE FANTASY STORIES OF GEORGE MACDONALD, editor Glenn Sadler has compiled a complete edition of MacDonald's shorter works, newly illustrated by artists Craig and Janet Yoe.

"I do not write," MacDonald once said, "for children, but for the childlike, whether of five, or fifty, or seventy-five." Here, then, for the childlike of all ages, is a collection of fairy tales and stories certain to delight both confirmed MacDonald readers and those about to meet him for the first time.

THE LIGHT PRINCESS

I: WHAT! NO CHILDREN?

ONCE upon a time, so long ago that I have quite forgotten the date, there lived a king and queen who had no children.

And the king said to himself, "All the queens of my acquaintance have children, some three, some seven, and some as many as twelve; and my queen has not one. I feel ill-used." So he made up his mind to be cross with his wife about it. But she bore it all like a good patient queen as she was. Then the king grew very cross indeed. But the queen pretended to take it all as a joke, and a very good one too.

"Why don't you have any daughters, at least?" said he. "I don't say *sons;* that might be too much to expect."

"I am sure, dear king, I am very sorry," said the queen.

"So you ought to be," retorted the king; "you are not going to make a virtue of *that*, surely."

But he was not an ill-tempered king, and in any matter of less moment would have let the queen have her own way with all his heart. This, however, was an affair of state.

The queen smiled.

"You must have patience with a lady, you know, dear king," said she.

She was, indeed a very nice queen, and heartily sorry that she could not oblige the king immediately.

Reprinted from *Adela Cathcart* (1864).

The king tried to have patience, but he succeeded very badly. It was more than he deserved, therefore, when, at last, the queen gave him a daughter—as lovely a little princess as ever cried.

II: WON'T I, JUST?

THE day grew near when the infant must be christened. The king wrote all the invitations with his own hand. Of course somebody was forgotten.

Now it does not generally matter if somebody *is* forgotten, only you must mind who. Unfortunately, the king forgot without intending to forget; and so the chance fell upon the Princess Makemnoit, which was awkward. For the princess was the king's own sister; and he ought not to have forgotten her. But she had made herself so disagreeable to the old king, their father, that he had forgotten her in making his will; and so it was no wonder that her brother forgot her in writing his invitations. But poor relations don't do anything to keep you in mind of them. Why don't they? The king could not see into the garret she lived in, could he?

She was a sour, spiteful creature. The wrinkles of contempt crossed the wrinkles of peevishness, and made her face as full of wrinkles as a pat of butter. If ever a king could be justified in forgetting anybody, this king was justified in forgetting his sister, even at a christening. She looked very odd, too. Her forehead was as large as all the rest of her face, and projected over it like a precipice. When she was angry, her little eyes flashed blue. When she hated anybody, they shone yellow and green. What they looked like when she loved anybody, I do not know; for I never heard of her loving anybody but herself, and I do not think she could have managed that if she had not somehow got used to herself. But what made it highly imprudent in the king to forget her was—that she was awfully clever. In fact, she was a witch; and when she bewitched anybody, he very soon had enough of it; for she beat all the wicked fairies in wickedness, and all the clever ones in cleverness. She despised all the modes we read of in history, in which offended fairies and witches have taken their revenges; and therefore, after waiting and waiting in vain for an invitation, she made up her mind at last to go without one, and make the whole family miserable, like a princess as she was.

So she put on her best gown, went to the palace, was kindly received by the happy monarch, who forgot that he had forgotten her, and took her place in the procession to the royal chapel. When they were all gathered about the font, she contrived to get next to it, and throw something into the water; after which she maintained a very respectful demeanour till the water was applied to the child's face. But at that moment she turned round in her place three times, and muttered the following words, loud enough for those beside her to hear: —

"Light of spirit, by my charms,
Light of body every part,
Never weary human arms —
Only crush thy parents' heart!"

They all thought she had lost her wits, and was repeating some foolish nursery rhyme; but a shudder went through the whole of them notwithstanding. The baby, on the contrary, began to laugh and crow; while the nurse gave a start and a smothered cry, for she thought she was struck with paralysis: she could not feel the baby in her arms. But she clasped it tight and said nothing.

The mischief was done.

III: SHE CAN'T BE OURS

HER atrocious aunt had deprived the child of all her gravity. If you ask me how this was effected

I answer, "In the easiest way in the world. She had only to destroy gravitation." For the princess was a philosopher, and knew all the *ins* and *outs* of the laws of gravitation as well as the *ins* and *outs* of her boot-lace. And being a witch as well, she could abrogate those laws in a moment; or at least so clog their wheels and rust their bearings, that they would not work at all. But we have more to do with what followed than with how it was done.

The first awkwardness that resulted from this unhappy privation was, that the moment the nurse began to float the baby up and down, she flew from her arms towards the ceiling. Happily, the resistance of the air brought her ascending career to a close within a foot of it. There she remained, horizontal as when she left her nurse's arms, kicking and laughing amazingly. The nurse in terror flew to the bell, and begged the footman, who answered it, to bring up the house-steps directly. Trembling in every limb, she climbed upon the steps, and had to stand upon the very top, and reach up, before she could catch the floating tail of the baby's long clothes.

When the strange fact came to be known, there was a terrible commotion in the palace. The occasion of its discovery by the king was naturally a repetition of the nurse's experience. Astonished that he felt no weight when the child was laid in his arms, he began to wave her up and—not down; for she slowly ascended to the ceiling as before, and there remained floating in perfect comfort and satisfaction, as was testified by her peals of tiny laughter. The king stood staring up in speechless amazement, and trembled so that his beard shook like grass in the wind. At last, turning to the queen, who was just as horror-struck as himself, he said, gasping, staring, and stammering,—

"She *can't* be ours, queen!"

Now the queen was much cleverer than the king, and had begun already to suspect that "this effect defective came by cause."

"I am sure she is ours," answered she. "But we ought to have taken better care of her at the christening. People who were never invited ought not to have been present."

"Oh, ho!" said the king, tapping his forehead with his forefinger, "I have it all. I've found out. Don't you see it, queen? Princess Makemnoit has bewitched her."

"That's just what I say," answered the queen.

"I beg your pardon, my love; I did not hear you. — John! bring the steps I get on my throne with."

For he was a little king with a great throne, like many other kings.

The throne-steps were brought, and set upon the dining-table, and John got upon the top of them. But he could not reach the little princess, who lay like a baby-laughter-cloud in the air, exploding continuously.

"Take the tongs, John," said his majesty; and getting up on the table, he handed them to him.

John could reach the baby now, and the little princess was handed down by the tongs.

IV: WHERE IS SHE?

ONE fine summer day, a month after these her first adventures, during which time she had been very carefully watched, the princess was lying on the bed in the queen's own chamber, fast asleep. One of the windows was open, for it was noon, and the day was so sultry that the little girl was wrapped in nothing less ethereal than slumber itself. The queen came into the room, and not observing that the baby was on the bed, opened another window. A frolicsome fairy wind, which had been watching for a chance of mischief, rushed in at the one window, and taking its

*John could not reach the little princess,
who lay like a baby-laughter-cloud in the air,
exploding continuously.*

way over the bed where the child was lying, caught her up, and rolling and floating her along like a piece of flue, or a dandelion seed, carried her with it through the opposite window, and away. The queen went down-stairs, quite ignorant of the loss she had herself occasioned.

When the nurse returned, she supposed that her majesty had carried her off, and, dreading a scolding, delayed making inquiry about her. But hearing nothing, she grew uneasy, and went at length to the queen's boudoir, where she found her majesty.

"Please, your majesty, shall I take the baby?" said she.

"Where is she?" asked the queen.

"Please forgive me. I know it was wrong."

"What do you mean?" said the queen, looking grave.

"Oh! don't frighten me, your majesty!" exclaimed the nurse, clasping her hands.

The queen saw that something was amiss, and fell down in a faint. The nurse rushed about the palace, screaming, "My baby! my baby!"

Every one ran to the queen's room. But the queen could give no orders. They soon found out, however, that the princess was missing, and in a moment the palace was like a beehive in a garden; and in one minute more the queen was brought to herself by a great shout and a clapping of hands. They had found the princess fast asleep under a rose-bush, to which the elvish little wind-puff had carried her, finishing its mischief by shaking a shower of red rose-leaves all over the little white sleeper. Startled by the noise the servants made, she woke, and furious with glee, scattered the rose-leaves in all directions, like a shower of spray in the sunset.

She was watched more carefully after this, no doubt; yet it would be endless to relate all the odd incidents resulting from this peculiarity of the young princess. But there never was a baby in a house, not

to say a palace, that kept the household in such constant good humour, at least below-stairs. If it was not easy for her nurses to hold her, at least she made neither their arms nor their hearts ache. And she was so nice to play at ball with! There was positively no danger of letting her fall. They might throw her down, or knock her down, or push her down, but couldn't *let* her down. It is true, they might let her fly into the fire or the coal-hole, or through the window; but none of these accidents had happened as yet. If you heard peals of laughter resounding from some unknown region, you might be sure enough of the cause. Going down into the kitchen, or *the room*, you would find Jane and Thomas, and Robert and Susan, all and sum, playing at ball with the little princess. She was the ball herself, and did not enjoy it the less for that. Away she went, flying from one to another, screeching with laughter. And the servants loved the ball itself better even than the game. But they had to take some care how they threw her, for if she received an upward direction she would never come down again without being fetched.

V: WHAT IS TO BE DONE?

BUT above-stairs it was different. One day, for instance, after breakfast, the king went into his counting-house, and counted out his money.

The operation gave him no pleasure.

"To think," said he to himself, "that every one of these gold sovereigns weighs a quarter of an ounce, and my real, live, flesh-and-blood princess weighs nothing at all!"

And he hated his gold sovereigns, as they lay with a broad smile of self-satisfaction all over their yellow faces.

The queen was in the parlour, eating bread and honey. But at the second mouthful she burst out crying, and could not swallow it. The king heard her sobbing. Glad of anybody, but especially of his queen, to quarrel with, he clashed his gold sovereigns into his money-box, clapped his crown on his head, and rushed into the parlour.

"What is all this about?" exclaimed he. "What are you crying for, queen?"

"I can't eat it," said the queen, looking ruefully at the honey-pot.

"No wonder!" retorted the king. "You've just eaten your breakfast—two turkey eggs, and three anchovies."

"Oh, that's not it!" sobbed her majesty. "It's my child, my child!"

"Well, what's the matter with your child? She's neither up the chimney nor down the draw-well. Just hear her laughing."

Yet the king could not help a sigh, which he tried to turn into a cough, saying,—

"It is a good thing to be light-hearted, I am sure, whether she be ours or not."

"It is a bad thing to be light-headed," answered the

queen, looking with prophetic soul far into the future.

"'Tis a good thing to be light-handed," said the king.

"'Tis a bad thing to be light-fingered," answered the queen.

"'Tis a good thing to be light-footed," said the king.

"'Tis a bad thing—" began the queen; but the king interrupted her.

"In fact," said he, with the tone of one who concludes an argument in which he has had only imaginary opponents, and in which, therefore, he has come off triumphant—"in fact, it is a good thing altogether to be light-bodied."

"But it is a bad thing altogether to be light-minded," retorted the queen, who was beginning to lose her temper.

This last answer quite discomfited his majesty, who turned on his heel, and betook himself to his counting-house again. But he was not half-way towards it, when the voice of his queen overtook him.

"And it's a bad thing to be light-haired," screamed she, determined to have more last words, now that her spirit was roused.

The queen's hair was black as night; and the king's had been, and his daughter's was, golden as morning. But it was not this reflection on his hair that arrested him; it was the double use of the word *light*. For the king hated all witticisms, and punning especially. And besides, he could not tell whether the queen meant light-*haired* or light-*heired*; for why might she not aspirate her vowels when she was ex-asperated herself?

He turned upon his other heel, and rejoined her. She looked angry still, because she knew that she was guilty, or, what was much the same, knew that he thought so.

"My dear queen," said he, "duplicity of any sort is exceedingly objectionable between married people of any rank, not to say kings and queens; and the most objectionable form duplicity can assume is that of punning."

"There!" said the queen, "I never made a jest, but I broke it in the making. I am the most unfortunate woman in the world!"

She looked so rueful, that the king took her in his arms; and they sat down to consult.

"Can you bear this?" said the king.

"No, I can't," said the queen.

"Well, what's to be done?" said the king.

"I'm sure I don't know," said the queen. "But might you not try an apology?"

"To my older sister, I suppose you mean?" said the king.

"Yes," said the queen.

"Well, I don't mind," said the king.

So he went the next morning to the house of the princess, and, making a very humble apology, begged her to undo the spell. But the princess declared, with a grave face, that she knew nothing at all about it. Her eyes, however, shone pink, which was a sign that she was happy. She advised the king and queen to have patience, and to mend their ways. The king returned disconsolate. The queen tried to comfort him.

"We will wait till she is older. She may then be able to suggest something herself. She will know at least how she feels, and explain things to us."

"But what if she should marry?" exclaimed the king, in sudden consternation at the idea.

"Well, what of that?" rejoined the queen.

"Just think! If she were to have children! In the course of a hundred years the air might be as full of floating children as of gossamers in autumn."

"That is no business of ours," replied the queen. "Besides, by that time they will have learned to take care of themselves."

A sigh was the king's only answer.

He would have consulted the court physicians; but he was afraid they would try experiments upon her.

VI: SHE LAUGHS TOO MUCH

EANTIME, notwithstanding awkward occurrences, and griefs that she brought upon her parents, the little princess laughed and grew—not fat, but plump and tall. She reached the age of seventeen, without having fallen into any worse scrape than a chimney; by rescuing her from which, a little bird-nesting urchin got fame and a black face. Nor, thoughtless as she was, had she committed anything worse than laughter at everybody and everything that came in her way. When she was told, for the sake of experiment, that General Clanrunfort was cut to pieces with all his troops, she laughed; when she heard that the enemy was on his way to besiege her papa's capital, she laughed hugely; but when she was told that the city would certainly be abandoned to the mercy of the enemy's soldiery—why, then she laughed immoderately. She never could be brought to see the serious side of anything. When her mother cried, she said,—

"What queer faces mamma makes! And she squeezes water out of her cheeks! Funny mamma!"

And when her papa stormed at her, she laughed, and danced round and round him, clapping her hands, and crying—

"Do it again, papa. Do it again! It's such fun! Dear, funny papa!"

And if he tried to catch her, she glided from him in an instant, not in the least afraid of him, but thinking it part of the game not to be caught. With one push of her foot, she would be floating in the air above his head; or she would go dancing backwards and forwards and sideways, like a great butterfly. It happened several times, when her father and mother were holding a consultation about her in private, that they were interrupted by vainly repressed outbursts of laughter over their heads; and looking up with indignation, saw her floating at full length in the air above them, whence she regarded them with the most comical appreciation of the position.

One day an awkward accident happened. The princess had come out upon the lawn with one of her attendants, who held her by the hand. Spying her father at the other side of the lawn, she snatched her hand from the maid's, and sped across to him. Now when she wanted to run alone, her custom was to catch up a stone in each hand, so that she might come down again after a bound. Whatever she wore as part of her attire had no effect in this way; even gold, when it thus became as it were a part of herself, lost all its weight for the time. But whatever she only held in her hands retained its downward tendency. On this occasion she could see nothing to catch up but a huge toad, that was walking across the lawn as if he had a hundred years to do it in. Not knowing what disgust meant, for this was one of her peculiarities, she snatched up the toad and bounded away. She had almost reached her father, and he was holding out his arms to receive her, and take from her lips the kiss which hovered on them like a butterfly on a rosebud, when a puff of wind blew her aside into the arms of a young page, who had just been receiving a message from his majesty. Now it was no great peculiarity in the princess that, once she was set agoing, it always cost her time and trouble to check herself. On this occasion there was not time. She *must* kiss—and she kissed the page. She did not mind it much; for she had no shyness in her composition; and she knew, besides, that she could not help it. So she only laughed, like a musical box. The poor page fared the worst. For the princess, trying to correct the unfortunate tendency of the kiss, put out her hands to keep her off the page; so that, along with the kiss, he received, on the other cheek, a slap with the huge black toad, which she poked right into his eye. He tried to laugh, too, but the attempt resulted in such an odd contortion of countenance, as showed that there was no danger of his pluming himself on the kiss. As for the king, his dignity was greatly hurt, and he did not speak to the page for a whole month.

I may here remark that it was very amusing to see her run, if her mode of progression would properly be called running. For first she would make a bound; then, having alighted, she would run a few steps, and make another bound. Sometimes she would fancy she had reached the ground before she actually had, and her feet would go backwards and forwards, running upon nothing at all, like those of a chicken on its back. Then she would laugh like the very spirit of fun; only in her laugh there was something missing. What it was, I find myself unable to describe. I think it was a certain tone, depending upon the possibility of sorrow—*morbidezza*, perhaps. She never smiled.

VII: TRY METAPHYSICS

AFTER a long avoidance of the painful subject, the king and queen resolved to hold a council of three upon it; and so they sent for the princess. In she came, sliding and flitting and gliding from one piece of furniture to another, and put herself at last in an arm-chair, in a sitting posture. Whether she could be said *to sit*, seeing she received no support from the seat of the chair, I do not pretend to determine.

"My dear child," said the king, "you must be aware by this time that you are not exactly like other people."

"Oh, you dear funny papa! I have got a nose, and two eyes, and all the rest. So have you. So has mamma."

"Now be serious, my dear, for once," said the queen.

"No, thank you, mamma; I had rather not."

"Would you not like to be able to walk like other people?" said the king.

"No indeed, I should think not. You only crawl. You are such slow coaches!"

"How do you feel, my child?" he resumed, after a pause of discomfiture.

"Quite well, thank you."

"I mean, what do you feel like?"

"Like nothing at all, that I know of."

"You must feel like something."

"I feel like a princess with such a funny papa, and such a dear pet of a queen-mamma!"

"Now really!" began the queen; but the princess interrupted her.

"Oh yes," she added, "I remember. I have a curious feeling sometimes, as if I were the only person that had any sense in the whole world."

She had been trying to behave herself with dignity; but now she burst into a violent fit of laughter, threw herself backwards over the chair, and went rolling about the floor in an ecstasy of enjoyment. The king picked her up easier than one does a down quilt, and replaced her in her former relation to the chair. The exact preposition expressing this relation I do not happen to know.

"Is there nothing you wish for?" resumed the king, who had learned by this time that it was useless to be angry with her.

"Oh, you dear papa!—yes," answered she.

"What is it, my darling?"

"I have been longing for it—oh, such a time!—ever since last night."

"Tell me what it is."

"Will you promise to let me have it?"

The king was on the point of saying *Yes*, but the wiser queen checked him with a single motion of her head.

"Tell me what it is first," said he.

"No no. Promise first."

"I dare not. What is it?"

"Mind, I hold you to your promise.—It is—-to be tied to the end of a string—a very long string indeed, and be flown like a kite. Oh such fun! I would rain rose-water, and hail sugar-plums, and snow whipped-cream, and—and—and—"

A fit of laughing checked her; and she would have been off again over the floor, had not the king started up and caught her just in time. Seeing that nothing but talk could be got out of her, he rang the bell, and sent her away with two of her ladies-in-waiting.

"Now, queen," he said, turning to her majesty, "what *is* to be done?"

"There is but one thing left," answered she. "Let us consult the college of Metaphysicians."

"Bravo!" cried the king; "we will."

Now at the head of this college were two very wise Chinese philosophers—by name Hum-Drum, and Kopy-Keck. For them the king sent; and straightway they came. In a long speech he communicated to them what they knew very well already—as who did not?—namely, the peculiar condition of his daughter in relation to the globe on which she dwelt; and requested them to consult together as to what might be the cause and probable cure of her *infirmity*. The king laid stress upon the word, but failed to discover his own pun. The queen laughed; but Hum-Drum and Kopy-Keck heard with humility and retired in silence.

Their consultation consisted chiefly in propounding and supporting, for the thousandth time, each his favourite theories. For the condition of the princess afforded delightful scope for the discussion of every question arising from the division of thought—in fact, of all the Metaphysics of the Chinese Empire. But it is only justice to say that they did not altogether neglect the discussion of the practical question, *what was to be done*.

Hum-Drum was a Materialist, and Kopy-Keck was a Spiritualist. The former was slow and sententious; the latter was quick and flighty: the latter had generally the first word; the former the last.

"I reassert my former assertion," began Kopy-Keck, with a plunge. "There is not a fault in the princess, body or soul; only they are wrong put together. Listen to me now, Hum-Drum, and I will tell you in brief what I think. Don't speak. Don't answer me. I *won't* hear you till I have done. —At that decisive moment, when souls seek their appointed habitations, two eager souls met, struck, rebounded, lost their way, and arrived each at the wrong place. The soul of the princess was one of those, and she went far astray. She does not belong by rights to this world at all, but to some other planet, probably Mercury. Her proclivity to her true sphere destroys all the natural influence which this orb would otherwise possess over her corporeal frame. She cares for nothing here. There is no relation between her and this world.

"She must therefore be taught, by the sternest compulsion, to take an interest in the earth as the earth. She must study every department of its history—its animal history; its vegetable history; its mineral history; its social history; its moral history; its political history; its scientific history; its literary history; its musical history; its artistical history; above all, its metaphysical history. She must begin with the

Chinese dynasty and end with Japan. But first of all she must study geology, and especially the history of the extinct races of animals—their natures, their habits, their loves, their hates, their revenges. She must—"

"Hold, h-o-o-old!" roared Hum-Drum. "It is certainly my turn now. My rooted and insubvertible conviction is, that the causes of the anomalies evident in the princess's condition are strictly and solely physical. But that is only tantamount to acknowledging that they exist. Hear my opinion.—From some cause or other, of no importance to our inquiry, the motion of her heart has been reversed. That remarkable combination of the suction and force-pump works the wrong way—I mean in the case of the unfortunate princess: it draws in where it should force out, and forces out where it should draw in. The offices of the auricles and the ventricles are subverted. The blood is sent forth by the veins, and returns by the arteries. Consequently it is running the wrong way through all her corporeal organism—lungs and all. Is it then at all mysterious, seeing that such is the case, that on the other particular of gravitation as well, she should differ from normal humanity? My proposal for the cure is this:—

"Phlebotomize until she is reduced to the last point of safety. Let it be effected, if necessary, in a warm bath. When she is reduced to a state of perfect asphyxy, apply a ligature to the left ankle, drawing it as tight as the bone will bear. Apply, at the same moment, another of equal tension around the right wrist. By means of plates constructed for the purpose, place the other foot and hand under the receivers of two air-pumps. Exhaust the receivers. Exhibit a pint of French brandy, and await the result.

"Which would presently arrive in the form of grim Death," said Kopy-Keck.

"If it should, she would yet die in doing our duty," retorted Hum-Drum.

But their majesties had too much tenderness for their volatile offspring to subject her to either of the schemes of the equally unscrupulous philosophers. Indeed, the most complete knowledge of the laws of nature would have been unserviceable in her case; for it was impossible to classify her. She was a fifth imponderable body, sharing all the other properties of the ponderable.

VIII: TRY A DROP OF WATER

PERHAPS the best thing for the princess would have been to fall in love. But how a princess who had no gravity could fall into anything is a difficulty— perhaps *the* difficulty. As for her own feelings on the subject, she did not even know that there was such a beehive of honey and stings to be fallen into. But now I come to mention another curious fact about her.

The palace was built on the shores of the loveliest lake in the world; and the princess loved this lake more than father or mother. The root of this prefer- ence no doubt, although the princess did not recog- nise it as such, was, that the moment she got into it, she recovered the natural right of which she had been so wickedly deprived—namely, gravity. Whether this was owing to the fact that water had been employed as the means of conveying the injury, I do not know. But it is certain that she could swim and dive like the duck that her old nurse said she was. The manner in which this alleviation of her misfortune was discov- ered was as follows.

One summer evening, during the carnival of the country, she had been taken upon the lake by the king and queen, in the royal barge. They were accom-

panied by many of the courtiers in a fleet of little
boats. In the middle of the lake she wanted to get into
the lord chancellor's barge, for his daughter, who was
a great favourite with her, was in it with her father.
Now though the old king rarely condescended to make
light of his misfortune, yet, happening on this occasion to be in a particularly good humour, as the barges
approached each other, he caught up the princess to
throw her into the chancellor's barge. He lost his
balance, however, and dropping into the bottom of
the barge, lost his hold of his daughter; not, however,
before imparting to her the downward tendency of his
own person, though in a somewhat different direction; for, as the king fell into the boat, she fell into
the water. With a burst of delighted laughter she disappeared in the lake. A cry of horror ascended from
the boats. They had never seen the princess go down
before. Half the men were under water in a moment;
but they had all, one after another, come up to the
surface again for breath, when—tinkle, tinkle, bab-
ble, and gush! came the princess's laugh over the
water from far away. There she was, swimming like
a swan. Nor would she come out for king or queen,
chancellor or daughter. She was perfectly obstinate.

But at the same time she seemed more sedate than
usual. Perhaps that was because a great pleasure
spoils laughing. At all events, after this, the passion
of her life was to get into the water, and she was
always the better behaved and the more beautiful the
more she had of it. Summer and winter it was quite
the same; only she could not stay so long in the water
when they had to break the ice to let her in. Any day,
from morning till evening in summer, she might be
descried—a streak of white in the blue water—lying
as still as the shadow of a cloud, or shooting along
like a dolphin; disappearing, and coming up again far
off, just where one did not expect her. She would

have been in the lake of a night too, if she could have had her way; for the balcony of her window overhung a deep pool in it; and through a shallow reedy passage she could have swum out into the wide wet water, and no one would have been any the wiser. Indeed, when she happened to wake in the moonlight, she could hardly resist the temptation. But there was the sad difficulty of getting into it. She had as great a dread of the air as some children have of the water. For the slightest gust of wind would blow her away; and a gust might arise in the stillest moment. And if she gave herself a push towards the water and just failed of reaching it, her situation would be dreadfully awkward, irrespective of the wind; for at best there she would have to remain, suspended in her night-gown, till she was seen and angled for by somebody from the window.

"Oh! if I had my gravity," thought she, contemplating the water, "I would flash off this balcony like a long white sea-bird, headlong into the darling wetness. Heigh-ho!"

This was the only consideration that made her wish to be like other people.

Another reason for her being fond of the water was that in it alone she enjoyed any freedom. For she could not walk out without a *cortége*, consisting in part of a troop of light-horses, for fear of the liberties which the wind might take with her. And the king grew more apprehensive with increasing years, till at last he would not allow her to walk abroad at all without some twenty silken cords fastened to as many parts of her dress, and held by twenty noblemen. Of course horseback was out of the question. But she bade good-bye to all this ceremony when she got into the water.

And so remarkable were its effects upon her, especially in restoring her for the time to the ordinary human gravity, that Hum-Drum and Kopy-Keck agreed in recommending the king to bury her alive for three years; in the hope that, as the water did her so much good, the earth would do her yet more. But the king had some vulgar prejudices against the experiment, and would not give his consent. Foiled in this, they yet agreed in another recommendation; which, seeing that one imported his opinions from China and the other from Tibet, was very remarkable indeed. They argued that, if water of external origin and application could be so efficacious, water from a deeper source might work a perfect cure; in short, that if the poor afflicted princess could by any means be made to cry, she might recover her lost gravity.

But how was this to be brought about? Therein lay all the difficulty—to meet which the philosophers were not wise enough. To make the princess cry was as impossible as to make her weigh. They sent for a professional beggar; commanded him to prepare his most touching oracle of woe; helped him out of the court charade-box, to whatever he wanted for dressing up, and promised great rewards in the event of his success. But it was all in vain. She listened to the mendicant artist's story, and gazed at his marvellous make-up, till she could contain herself no longer, and went into the most undignified contortions for relief, shrieking, positively screeching with laughter.

When she had a little recovered herself, she ordered her attendants to drive him away, and not give him a single copper; whereupon his look of mortified discomfiture wrought her punishment and his revenge, for it sent her into violent hysterics, from which she was with difficulty recovered.

But so anxious was the king that the suggestion should have a fair trial, that he put himself in a rage one day, and, rushing up to her room, gave her an awful whipping. Yet not a tear would flow. She looked grave, and her laughing sounded uncommonly like screaming—that was all. The good old tyrant, though he put on his best gold spectacles to look, could not discover the smallest cloud in the serene blue of her eyes.

IX: PUT ME IN AGAIN

IT must have been about this time that the son of a king, who lived a thousand miles from Lagobel, set out to look for the daughter of a queen. He travelled far and wide, but as sure as he found a princess, he found some fault in her. Of course he could not marry a mere woman, however beautiful; and there was no princess to be found worthy of him. Whether the prince was so near perfection that he had a right to demand perfection itself, I cannot pretend to say. All I know is, that he was a fine, handsome, brave, generous, well-bred, and well-behaved youth, as all princes are.

In his wanderings he had come across some reports about our princess; but as everybody said she was bewitched, he never dreamed that she could bewitch him. For what indeed could a prince do with a princess that had lost her gravity? Who could tell what she might not lose next? She might lose her visibilty, or her tangibility; or, in short, the power of making impressions upon the radical sensorium; so that he should never be able to tell whether she was dead or alive. Of course he made no further inquiries about her.

One day he lost sight of his retinue in a great forest. These forests are very useful in delivering princes from their courtiers, like a sieve that keeps back the bran. Then the princes get away to follow their fortunes. In this they have the advantage of the princesses, who are forced to marry before they have had a bit of fun. I wish our princesses got lost in a forest sometimes.

One lovely evening, after wandering about for many days, he found that he was approaching the outskirts of this forest; for the trees had got so thin that he could see the sunset through them; and he soon came upon a kind of heath. Next he came upon signs of human neighbourhood; but by this time it was getting late, and there was nobody in the fields to direct him.

After travelling for another hour, his horse, quite worn out with long labour and lack of food, fell, and was unable to rise again. So he continued his journey on foot. At length he entered another wood—not a wild forest, but a civilized wood, through which a footpath led him to the side of a lake. Along this path the prince pursued his way through the gathering darkness. Suddenly he paused, and listened. Strange sounds came across the water. It was, in fact, the princess laughing. Now there was something odd in her laugh, as I have already hinted; for the hatching of a real hearty laugh requires the incubation of gravity; and perhaps this was how the prince mistook the laughter for screaming. Looking over the lake, he saw something white in the water; and, in an instant, he had torn off his tunic, kicked off his sandals, and plunged in. He soon reached the white object, and found that it was a woman. There was not light enough to show that she was a princess, but quite enough to show that she was a lady, for it does not want much light to see that.

Now I cannot tell how it came about,—whether she pretended to be drowning, or whether he frightened her, or caught her so as to embarrass her,—but certainly he brought her to shore in a fashion ignominious to a swimmer, and more nearly drowned than she had ever expected to be; for the water had got into her throat as often as she had tried to speak.

At the place to which he bore her, the bank was only a foot or two above the water; so he gave her a strong lift out of the water, to lay her on the bank. But, her gravitation ceasing the moment she left the water, away she went up into the air, scolding and screaming.

"You naughty, *naughty*, NAUGHTY, *NAUGHTY* man!" she cried.

No one had ever succeeded in putting her into a passion before.—When the prince saw her ascend, he thought he must have been bewitched, and have mistaken a great swan for a lady. But the princess caught hold of the topmost cone upon a lofty fir. This came off; but she caught at another; and, in fact, stopped herself by gathering cones, dropping them as the stalks gave way. The prince, meantime, stood in the water, staring, and forgetting to get out. But the princess disappearing, he scrambled on shore, and went in the direction of the tree. There he found her climbing down one of the branches towards the stem. But in the darkness of the wood, the prince continued in some bewilderment as to what the phenomenon could be; until, reaching the ground, and seeing him standing there, she caught hold of him, and said,—

"I'll tell papa."

"Oh no, you won't!" returned the prince.

"Yes, I will," she persisted. "What business had you to pull me down out of the water, and throw me to the bottom of the air? I never did you any harm."

"Pardon me. I did not mean to hurt you."

"I don't believe you have any brains; and that is a worse loss than your wretched gravity. I pity you."

The prince now saw that he had come upon the bewitched princess, and had already offended her. But before he could think what to say next, she burst out angrily, giving a stamp with her foot that would have sent her aloft again but for the hold she had of his arm,—

"Put me up directly."

"Put you up where, you beauty?" asked the prince.

He had fallen in love with her almost, already; for her anger made her more charming than any one else had ever beheld her; and, as far as he could see, which certainly was not far, she had not a single fault about her, except, of course, that she had not any gravity. No prince, however, would judge of a princess by weight. The loveliness of her foot he would hardly estimate by the depth of the impression it could make in mud.

"Put you up where, you beauty?" asked the prince.

"In the water, you stupid!" answered the princess.

"Come, then," said the prince.

The condition of her dress, increasing her usual difficulty in walking, compelled her to cling to him; and he could hardly persuade himself that he was not in a delightful dream, notwithstanding the torrent of musical abuse with which she overwhelmed him. The prince being therefore in no hurry, they came upon the lake at quite another part, where the bank was twenty-five feet high at least; and when they had reached the edge, he turned towards the princess, and said,—

"How am I to put you in?"

"That is your business," she answered, quite snappishly. "You took me out—put me in again."

"Very well," said the prince; and, catching her up in his arms, he sprang with her from the rock. The princess had just time to give one delighted shriek of laughter before the water closed over them. When they came to the surface, she found that, for a moment or two, she could not even laugh, for she had gone down with such a rush, that it was with diffi-

The water closed over them.

27

culty she recovered her breath. The instant they reached the surface—

"How do you like falling in?" said the prince.

After some effort the princess panted out,—

"Is that what you call *falling in?*"

"Yes, answered the prince, "I should think it a very tolerable specimen."

"It seemed to me like going up," rejoined she.

"My feeling was certainly one of elevation too," the prince conceded.

The princess did not appear to understand him, for she retorted his question:—

"How do *you* like falling in?" said the princess.

"Beyond everything," answered he; "for I have fallen in with the only perfect creature I ever saw."

"No more of that: I am tired of it," said the princess.

Perhaps she shared her father's aversion to punning.

"Don't you like falling in, then?" said the prince.

"It is the most delightful fun I ever had in my life," answered she. "I never fell before. I wish I could learn. To think I am the only person in my father's kingdom that can't fall!"

Here the poor princess looked almost sad.

"I shall be most happy to fall in with you any time you like," said the prince, devotedly.

"Thank you. I don't know. Perhaps it would not be proper. But I don't care. At all events, as we have fallen in, let us have a swim together."

"With all my heart," responded the prince.

And away they went, swimming, and diving, and floating, until at last they heard cries along the shore, and saw lights glancing in all directions. It was now quite late, and there was no moon.

"I must go home," said the princess. "I am very sorry, for this is delightful."

"So am I," returned the prince. "But I am glad I

haven't a home to go to—at least, I don't exactly know where it is."

"I wish I hadn't one either," rejoined the princess; "it is so stupid! I have a great mind," she continued, "to play them all a trick. Why couldn't they leave me alone? They won't trust me in the lake for a single night!—You see where that green light is burning? That is the window of my room. Now if you would just swim there with me very quietly, and when we are all but under the balcony, give me such a push— *up* you call it—as you did a little while ago, I should be able to catch hold of the balcony, and get in at the window; and then they may look for me till tomorrow morning!"

"With more obedience than pleasure," said the prince, gallantly; and away they swam, very gently.

"Will you be in the lake to-morrow night?" the prince ventured to ask.

"To be sure I will. I don't think so. Perhaps," was the princess's somewhat strange answer.

But the prince was intelligent enough not to press her further; and merely whispered, as he gave her the parting lift, "Don't tell." The only answer the princess returned was a rougish look. She was already a yard above his head. The look seemed to say, "Never fear. It is too good fun to spoil that way."

So perfectly like other people had she been in the water, that even yet the prince could scarcely believe his eyes when he saw her ascend slowly, grasp the balcony, and disappear through the window. He turned, almost expecting to see her still by his side. But he was alone in the water. So he swam away quietly, and watched the lights roving about the shore for hours after the princess was safe in her chamber. As soon as they disappeared, he landed in search of his tunic and sword, and, after some trouble, found them again. Then he made the best of his way round the lake to the other side. There the wood was wilder, and the shore steeper—rising more immediately towards the mountains which surrounded the lake on all sides, and kept sending it messages of silvery streams from morning to night, and all night long. He soon found a spot whence he could see the green light in the princess's room, and where, even in the broad daylight, he would be in no danger of being discovered from the opposite shore. It was a sort of cave in the rock, where he provided himself a bed of withered leaves, and lay down too tired for hunger to keep him awake. All night long he dreamed that he was swimming with the princess.

X: LOOK AT THE MOON

EARLY the next morning the prince set out to look for something to eat, which he soon found at a forester's hut, where for many following days he was supplied with all that a brave prince could consider necessary. And having plenty to keep him alive for the present, he would not think of wants not yet in existence. Whenever Care intruded, this prince always bowed him out in the most princely manner.

When he returned from his breakfast to his watch-cave, he saw the princess already floating about in the lake, attended by the king and queen—whom he knew by their crowns—and a great company in lovely little boats, with canopies of all the colours of the rainbow, and flags and streamers of a great many more. It was a very bright day, and soon the prince, burned up with the heat, began to long for the cold water and the cool princess. But he had to endure till twilight; for the boats had provisions on board, and it was not till the sun went down that the gay party began to vanish. Boat after boat drew away to the shore, following that of the king and queen, till only

one, apparently the princess's own boat, remained.
But she did not want to go home even yet, and the
prince thought he saw her order the boat to the shore
without her. At all events, it rowed away; and now,
of all the radiant company, only one white speck remained. Then the prince began to sing.

And this is what he sang:—

"Lady fair,
  Swan-white,
  Lift thine eyes,
  Banish night
  By the might
  Of thine eyes.

"Snowy arms,
  Oars of snow,
  Oar her hither,
  Plashing low.
  Soft and slow,
  Oar her hither.

"Stream behind her
  O'er the lake,
  Radiant whiteness!
  In her wake
  Following, following for her sake,
  Radiant whiteness!

"Cling about her,
  Waters blue;
  Part not from her,
  But renew

Cold and true
Kisses round her.

"Lap me round,
Waters sad
That have left her;
Make me glad,
For ye had
Kissed her ere ye left her."

Before he had finished his song, the princess was just under the place where he sat, and looking up to find him. Her ears had led her truly.

"Would you like a fall, princess?" said the prince, looking down.

"Ah! there you are! Yes, if you please, prince," said the princess, looking up.

"How do you know I am a prince, princess?" said the prince.

"Because you are a very nice young man, prince," said the princess.

"Come up then, princess."

"Fetch me, prince."

The prince took off his scarf, then his sword-belt, then his tunic, and tied them all together, and let them down. But the line was far too short. He unwound his turban, and added it to the rest, when it was all but long enough; and his purse completed it. The princess just managed to lay hold of the knot of money, and was beside him in a moment. This rock was much higher than the other, and the splash and the dive were tremendous. The princess was in ecstasies of delight, and their swim was delicious.

Night after night they met, and swam about in the dark clear lake; where such was the prince's gladness, that (whether the princess's way of looking at things infected him, or he was actually getting light-headed) he often fancied that he was swimming in the sky instead of the lake. But when he talked about being in heaven, the princess laughed at him dreadfully.

When the moon came, she brought them fresh pleasure. Everything looked strange and new in her light, with an old, withered, yet unfading newness. When the moon was nearly full, one of their great delights was to dive deep in the water, and then, turning round, look up through it at the great blot of light close above them, shimmering and trembling and wavering, spreading and contracting, seeming to melt away, and again grow solid. Then they would shoot up through the blot; and lo! there was the moon, far off, clear and steady and cold, and very lovely, at the bottom of a deeper and bluer lake than theirs, as the princess said.

The prince soon found out that while in the water the princess was very like other people. And besides this, she was not so forward in her questions or pert in her replies at sea as on shore. Neither did she laugh so much; and when she did laugh, it was more gently. She seemed altogether more modest and maidenly in the water than out of it. But when the prince, who had really fallen in love when he fell in the lake, began to talk to her about love, she always turned her head towards him and laughed. After a while she began to look puzzled, as if she were trying to understand what he meant, but could not—revealing a notion that he meant something. But as soon as ever she left the lake, she was so altered, that the prince said to himself, "If I marry her, I see no help for it: we must turn merman and mermaid, and go out to sea at once."

XI: HISS!

THE princess's pleasure in the lake had grown to a passion, and she could scarcely bear to be out of it for an hour. Imagine then her consternation, when, diving with the prince one night, a sudden suspicion seized her that the lake was not so deep as it used to be. The prince could not imagine what had happened. She shot to the surface, and, without a word, swam at full speed towards the higher side of the lake. He followed, begging to know if she was ill, or what was the matter. She never turned her head, or took the smallest notice of his question. Arrived at the shore, she coasted the rocks with minute inspection. But she was not able to come to a conclusion, for the moon was very small, and so she could not see well. She turned therefore and swam home, without saying a word to explain her conduct to the prince, of whose presence she seemed no longer conscious. He withdrew to his cave, in great perplexity and distress.

Next day she made many observations, which, alas! strengthened her fears. She saw that the banks were too dry; and that the grass on the shore, and the trailing plants on the rocks, were withering away. She caused marks to be made along the borders, and examined them, day after day, in all directions of the wind; till at last the horrible idea became a certain fact—that the surface of the lake was slowly sinking.

The poor princess nearly went out of the little mind she had. It was awful to her to see the lake, which she loved more than any living thing, lie dying before her eyes. It sank away, slowly vanishing. The tops of rocks that had never been seen till now, began to appear far down in the clear water. Before long they were dry in the sun. It was fearful to think of the mud that would soon lie there baking and festering, full of lovely creatures dying, and ugly creatures coming to life, like the unmaking of a world. And how hot the sun would be without any lake! She could not bear to swim in it any more, and began to pine away. Her life seemed bound up with it; and ever as the lake sank, she pined. People said she would not live an hour after the lake was gone.

But she never cried.

Proclamation was made to all the kingdom, that whosoever should discover the cause of the lake's decrease, would be rewarded after a princely fashion. Hum-Drum and Kopy-Keck applied themselves to their physics and metaphysics; but in vain. Not even they could suggest a cause.

Now the fact was that the old princess was at the root of the mischief. When she heard that her niece found more pleasure in the water than any one else had out of it, she went into a rage, and cursed herself for her want of foresight.

"But," said she, "I will soon set all right. The king and the people shall die of thirst; their brains shall boil and frizzle in their skulls before I will lose my revenge."

And she laughed a ferocious laugh, that made the hairs on the back of her black cat stand erect with terror.

Then she went to an old chest in the room, and opening it, took out what looked like a piece of dried seaweed. This she threw into a tub of water. Then she threw some powder into the water, and stirred it with her bare arm, muttering over it words of hideous sound, and yet more hideous import. Then she set the tub aside, and took from the chest a huge bunch of a hundred rusty keys, that clattered in her shaking hands. Then she sat down and proceeded to oil them all. Before she had finished, out from the tub, the water of which had kept on a slow motion ever since she had ceased stirring it, came the head and half the body of a huge gray snake. But the witch did not look round. It grew out of the tub, waving itself backwards and forwards with a slow horizontal motion, till it reached the princess, when it laid its head upon her shoulder, and gave a low hiss in her ear. She started— but with joy; and seeing the head resting on her shoulder, drew it towards her and kissed it. Then she drew it all out of the tub, and wound it round her body. It was one of those dreadful creatures which few have ever beheld—the White Snakes of Darkness.

Then she took the keys and went down to her cellar; and as she unlocked the door she said to herself,—

"This *is* worth living for!"

Locking the door behind her, she descended a few steps into the cellar, and crossing it, unlocked another door into a dark, narrow passage. She locked this also behind her, and descended a few more steps. If any one had followed the witch-princess, he would have heard her unlock exactly one hundred doors, and descend a few steps after unlocking each. When she had unlocked the last, she entered a vast cave, the roof of which was supported by huge natural pillars of rock. Now this room was the under side of the bottom of the lake.

She then untwined the snake from her body, and held it by the tail high above her. The hideous creature stretched up its head towards the roof of the cavern, which it was just able to reach. It then began to move its head backwards and forwards, with a slow oscillating motion, as if looking for something. At the same moment the witch began to walk round and round the cavern, coming nearer to the centre every circuit; while the head of the snake described the same path over the roof that she did over the floor, for she kept holding it up. And still it kept slowly oscillating. Round and round the cavern they went, ever lessening the circuit, till at last the snake made a sudden dart, and clung to the roof with its mouth.

"That's right, my beauty!" cried the princess; "drain it dry."

She let it go, left it hanging, and sat down on a great stone, with her black cat, which had followed her all round the cave, by her side. Then she began to knit and mutter awful words. The snake hung like a huge leech, sucking at the stone; the cat stood with his back arched, and his tail like a piece of cable, looking up at the snake; and the old woman sat and knitted and muttered. Seven days and seven nights they remained thus; when suddenly the serpent dropped from the roof as if exhausted, and shrivelled up till it was again like a piece of dried seaweed. The witch started to her feet, picked it up, put it in her pocket, and looked up at the roof. One drop of water was trembling on the spot where the snake had been sucking. As soon as she saw that, she turned and fled, followed by her cat. Shutting the door in a terrible hurry, she locked it, and having muttered some frightful words, sped to the next, which also she locked and muttered over; and so with all the hundred doors, till she arrived in her own cellar. There she sat down on the floor ready to faint, but listening with malicious delight to the rushing of the water, which she could hear distinctly through all the hundred doors.

But this was not enough. Now that she had tasted revenge, she lost her patience. Without further measures, the lake would be too long in disappearing. So the next night, with the last shred of the dying old moon rising, she took some of the water in which she had revived the snake, put it in a bottle, and set out, accompanied by her cat. Before morning she had made the entire circuit of the lake, muttering fearful

*The snake hung like a huge leech,
sucking at the stone.*

words as she crossed every stream, and casting into it some of the water out of her bottle. When she had finished the circuit she muttered yet again, and flung a handful of water towards the moon. Thereupon every spring in the country ceased to throb and bubble, dying away like the pulse of a dying man. The next day there was no sound of falling water to be heard along the borders of the lake. The very courses were dry; and the mountains showed no silvery streaks down their dark sides. And not alone had the fountains of mother Earth ceased to flow; for all the babies throughout the country were crying dreadfully— only without tears.

XII: WHERE IS THE PRINCE?

NEVER since the night when the princess left him so abruptly had the prince had a single interview with her. He had seen her once or twice in the lake; but as far as he could discover, she had not been in it any more at night. He had sat and sung, and looked in vain for his Nereid; while she, like a true Nereid, was wasting away with her lake, sinking as it sank, withering as it dried. When at length he discovered the change that was taking place in the level of the water, he was in great alarm and perplexity. He could not tell whether the lake was dying because the lady had forsaken it; or whether the lady would not come because the lake had begun to sink. But he resolved to know so much at least.

He disguised himself, and, going to the palace, requested to see the lord chamberlain. His appearance at once gained his request; and the lord chamberlain, being a man of some insight, perceived that there was more in the prince's solicitation than met the ear. He felt likewise that no one could tell whence a solution of the present difficulties might arise. So he granted the prince's prayer to be made shoe-black to the princess. It was rather cunning in the prince to request such an easy post, for the princess could not possibly soil as many shoes as other princesses.

He soon learned all that could be told about the princess. He went nearly distracted; but after roaming about the lake for days, and diving in every depth that remained, all that he could do was to put an extra polish on the dainty pair of boots that was never called for.

For the princess kept her room, with the curtains drawn to shut out the dying lake. But could not shut it out of her mind for a moment. It haunted her imagination so that she felt as if the lake were her soul, drying up within her, first to mud, then to madness and death. She thus brooded over the change, with all its dreadful accompaniments, till she was nearly distracted. As for the prince, she had forgotten him. However much she had enjoyed his company in the water, she did not care for him without it. But she seemed to have forgotten her father and mother too.

The lake went on sinking. Small slimy spots began to appear, which glittered steadily amidst the changeful shine of the water. These grew to broad patches of mud, which widened and spread, with rocks here and there, and floundering fishes and crawling eels swarming. The people went everywhere catching these, and looking for anything that might have dropped from the royal boats.

At length the lake was all but gone, only a few of the deepest pools remaining unexhausted.

It happened one day that a party of youngsters found themselves on the brink of one of these pools in the very centre of the lake. It was a rocky basin of considerable depth. Looking in, they saw at the bottom something that shone yellow in the sun. A little

boy jumped in and dived for it. It was a plate of gold
covered with writing. They carried it to the king.

On one side of it stood these words:—

"Death alone from death can save.
  Love is death, and so is brave.
  Love can fill the deepest grave.
  Love loves on beneath the wave."

Now this was enigmatical enough to the king and
courtiers. But the reverse of the plate explained it a
little. Its writing amounted to this:—

"If the lake should disappear, they must find the
hole through which the water ran. But it would be
useless to try to stop it by any ordinary means. There
was but one effectual mode.—The body of a living
man should alone stanch the flow. The man must
give himself of his own will; and the lake must take
his life as it filled. Otherwise the offering would be of
no avail. If the nation could not provide one hero, it
was time it should perish."

XIII: HERE I AM

THIS was a very disheartening revelation to the
king—not that he was unwilling to sacrifice a
subject, but that he was hopeless of finding a man
willing to sacrifice himself. No time was to be lost,
however, for the princess was lying motionless on
her bed, and taking no nourishment but lake-water,
which was now none of the best. Therefore the king
caused the contents of the wonderful plate of gold to
be published throughout the country.

No one, however, came forward.

The prince, having gone several days' journey into
the forest, to consult a hermit whom he had met there
on his way to Lagobel, knew nothing of the oracle till
his return.

When he had acquainted himself with all the particulars, he sat down and thought,—

"She will die if I don't do it, and life would be nothing to me without her; so I shall lose nothing by doing it. And life will be as pleasant to her as ever, for she will soon forget me. And there will be so much more beauty and happiness in the world!—To be sure, I shall not see it." (Here the poor prince gave a sigh.) "How lovely the lake will be in the moonlight, with that glorious creature sporting in it like a wild goddess!—It is rather hard to be drowned by inches, though. Let me see—that will be seventy inches of me to drown." (Here he tried to laugh, but could not.) "The longer the better, however," he resumed; "for can I not bargain that the princess shall be beside me all the time? So I shall see her once more, kiss her perhaps,—who knows? and die looking in her eyes. It will be no death. At least, I shall not feel it. And to see the lake filling for the beauty again!—All right! I am ready."

He kissed the princess's boot, laid it down, and hurried to the king's apartment. But feeling, as he went, that anything sentimental would be disagreeable, he resolved to carry off the whole affair with nonchalance. So he knocked at the door of the king's counting-house, where it was all but a capital crime to disturb him.

When the king heard the knock he started up, and opened the door in a rage. Seeing only the shoeblack, he drew his sword. This, I am sorry to say, was his usual mode of asserting his regality when he thought his dignity was in danger. But the prince was not in the least alarmed.

"Please your majesty, I'm your butler," said he.

"My butler! you lying rascal! What do you mean?"

"I mean, I will cork your big bottle."

"Is the fellow mad?" bawled the king, raising the point of his sword.

"I will put a stopper—plug—what you call it, in your leaky lake, grand monarch,"said the prince.

The king was in such a rage that before he could speak he had time to cool, and to reflect that it would be great waste to kill the only man who was willing to be useful in the present emergency, seeing that in the end the insolent fellow would be as dead as if he had died by his majesty's own hand.

"Oh!" said he at last, putting up his sword with difficulty, it was so long; "I am obliged to you, you young fool! Take a glass of wine?"

"No, thank you," replied the prince.

"Very well," said the king. "Would you like to run and see your parents before you make your experiment?"

"No, thank you," said the prince.

"Then we will go and look for the hole at once," said his majesty, and proceeded to call some attendants.

"Stop, please your majesty; I have a condition to make," interposed the prince.

"What!" exclaimed the king, "a condition! and with me! How dare you?"

"As you please," returned the prince, coolly. "I wish your majesty a good morning."

"You wretch! I will have you put in a sack, and stuck in the hole."

"Very well, your majesty," replied the prince, becoming a little more respectful, lest the wrath of the king should deprive him of the pleasure of dying for the princess. "But what good will that do your majesty? Please to remember that the oracle says the victim must offer himself."

"Well, you *have* offered yourself," retorted the king.

"Yes, upon one condition."

"Condition again!" roared the king, once more drawing his sword. "Begone! Somebody else will be glad enough to take the honour off your shoulders."

"Your majesty knows it will not be easy to get another to take my place."

"Well, what is your condition?" growled the king, feeling that the prince was right.

"Only this," replied the prince: "that, as I must on no account die before I am fairly drowned, and the waiting will be rather wearisome, the princess, your daughter, shall go with me, feed me with her own hands, and look at me now and then to comfort me; for you must confess it *is* rather hard. As soon as the water is up to my eyes, she may go and be happy, and forget her poor shoeblack."

Here the prince's voice faltered, and he very nearly grew sentimental, in spite of his resolution.

"Why didn't you tell me before what your condition was? Such a fuss about nothing!" exclaimed the king.

"Do you grant it?" persisted the prince.

"Of course I do," replied the king.

"Very well. I am ready."

"Go and have some dinner, then, while I set my people to find the place."

The king ordered out his guards, and gave directions to the officers to find the hole in the lake at once. So the bed of the lake was marked out in divisions and thoroughly examined, and in an hour or so the hole was discovered. It was in the middle of a stone, near the centre of the lake, in the very pool where the golden plate had been found. It was a three-cornered hole of no great size. There was water all round the stone, but very little was flowing through the hole.

XIV: THIS IS VERY KIND OF YOU

HE prince went to dress for the occasion, for he was resolved to die like a prince.

When the princess heard that a man had offered to die for her, she was so transported that she jumped off the bed, feeble as she was, and danced about the room for joy. She did not care who the man was; that was nothing to her. The hole wanted stopping; and if only a man would do, why, take one. In an hour or two more everything was ready. Her maid dressed her in haste, and they carried her to the side of the lake. When she saw it she shrieked, and covered her face with her hands. They bore her across to the stone, where they had already placed a little boat for her. The water was not deep enough to float it, but they hoped it would be, before long. They laid her on cushions, placed in the boat wines and fruits and other nice things, and stretched a canopy over all.

In a few minutes the prince appeared. The princess recognized him at once, but did not think it worthwhile to acknowledge him.

"Here I am," said the prince. "Put me in."

"They told me it was a shoeblack," said the princess.

"So I am," said the prince. "I black your little boots three times a day, because they were all I could get of you. Put me in."

The courtiers did not resent his bluntness, except by saying to each other that he was taking it out in impudence.

But how was he to be put in? The golden plate contained no instructions on this point. The prince looked at the hole, and saw but one way. He put both legs into it, sitting on the stone, and, stooping forward, covered the corner that remained open with his two hands. In this uncomfortable position he re-

45

solved to abide his fate, and turning to the people,
said,—

"Now you can go."

The king had already gone home to dinner.

"Now you can go," repeated the princess after him,
like a parrot.

The people obeyed her and went.

Presently a little wave flowed over the stone, and
wetted one of the prince's knees. But he did not mind
it much. He began to sing, and the song he sang was
this:—

"As a world that has no well,
Darkly bright in forest dell;
As a world without the gleam
Of the downward-going stream;
As a world without the glance
Of the ocean's fair expanse;
As a world where never rain
Glittered on the sunny plain;—
Such, my heart, thy world would be,
If no love did flow in thee.

"As a world without the sound
Of the rivulets underground;
Or the bubbling of the spring
Out of darkness wandering;
Or the mighty rush and flowing
Of the river's downward going;
Or the music-showers that drop
On the outspread beech's top;
Or the ocean's mighty voice,
When his lifted waves rejoice;—

Such, my soul, thy world would be,
If no love did sing in thee.

"*Lady, keep thy world's delight;*
  Keep the waters in thy sight.
  Love hath made me strong to go,
  For thy sake, to realms below,
  Where the water's shine and hum
  Through the darkness never come:
  Let, I pray, one thought of me
  Spring, a little well, in thee;
  Lest thy loveless soul be found
  Like a dry and thirsty ground."

"Sing again, prince. It makes it less tedious," said the princess.

But the prince was too much overcome to sing any more, and a long pause followed.

"This is very kind of you, prince," said the princess at last, quite coolly, as she lay in the boat with her eyes shut.

"I am sorry I can't return the compliment," thought the prince; "but you are worth dying for, after all."

Again a wavelet, and another, and another flowed over the stone, and wetted both the prince's knees; but he did not speak or move. Two—three—four hours passed in this way, the princess apparently asleep, and the prince very patient. But he was much disappointed in his position, for he had none of the consolation he had hoped for.

At last he could bear it no longer.

"Princess!" said he.

But at the moment up started the princess, crying,—

"I'm afloat! I'm afloat!"

And the little boat bumped against the stone.

"Princess!" repeated the prince, encouraged by seeing her wide awake and looking eagerly at the water.

"Well?" said she, without looking round.

"Your papa promised that you should look at me, and you haven't looked at me once."

"Did he? Then I suppose I must. But I am so sleepy!"

"Sleep then, darling, and don't mind me," said the poor prince.

"Really, you are very good," replied the princess. "I think I will go to sleep again."

"Just give me a glass of wine and a biscuit first," said the prince, very humbly.

"With all my heart," said the princess, and gaped as she said it.

She got the wine and the biscuit, however, and leaning over the side of the boat towards him, was compelled to look at him.

"Why, prince," she said, "you don't look well! Are your sure you don't mind it?"

"Not a bit," answered he, feeling very faint indeed. "Only I shall die before it is of any use to you, unless I have something to eat."

"There, then," said she, holding out the wine to him.

"Ah! you must feed me. I dare not move my hands. The water would run away directly."

"Good gracious!" said the princess; and she began at once to feed him with bits of biscuit and sips of wine.

As she fed him, he contrived to kiss the tips of her fingers now and then. She did not seem to mind it, one way or the other. But the prince felt better.

"Now, for your own sake, princess," said he, "I cannot let you go to sleep. You must sit and look at me, else I shall not be able to keep up."

"Well, I will do anything I can to oblige you," answered she, with condescension; and, sitting down, she did look at him, and kept looking at him with wonderful steadiness, considering all things.

The sun went down, and the moon rose, and, gush after gush, the waters were rising up the prince's body. They were up to his waist now.

"Why can't we go and have a swim?" said the princess. "There seems to be water enough just about here."

"I shall never swim more," said the prince.

"Oh, I forgot," said the princess, and was silent.

So the water grew and grew, and rose up and up on the prince. And the princess sat and looked at him. She fed him now and then. The night wore on. The waters rose and rose. The moon rose likewise higher and higher, and shone full on the face of the dying prince. The water was up to his neck.

"Will you kiss me, princess?" said he, feebly. The nonchalance was all gone now."

"Yes, I will," answered the princess, and kissed him with a long, sweet, cold kiss.

"Now," said he, with a sigh of content, "I die happy."

He did not speak again. The princess gave him some wine for the last time: he was past eating. Then she sat down again, and looked at him. The water rose and rose. It touched his chin. It touched his lower lip. It touched between his lips. He shut them hard to keep it out. The princess began to feel strange. It touched his upper lip. He breathed through his nostrils. The princess looked wild. It covered his nostrils. Her eyes looked scared, and shone strange in the moonlight. His head fell back; the water closed over it, and the bubbles of his last breath bubbled up through the water. The princess gave a shriek, and sprang into the lake.

She laid hold first of one leg, and then of the other,

and pulled and tugged, but she could not move either. She stopped to take breath, and that made her think that he could not get any breath. She was frantic. She got hold of him, and held his head above the water, which was possible now his hands were no longer on the hole. But it was of no use, for he was past breathing.

Love and water brought back all her strength. She got under the water, and pulled and pulled with her whole might, till at last she got one leg out. The other easily followed. How she got him into the boat she never could tell; but when she did, she fainted away. Coming to herself, she seized the oars, kept herself steady as best she could, and rowed and rowed, though she had never rowed before. Round rocks, and over shallows, and through mud she rowed, till she got to the landing-stairs of the palace. By this time her people were on the shore, for they had heard her shriek. She made them carry the prince to her own room, and lay him in her bed, and light a fire, and send for the doctors.

"But the lake, your highness!" said the chamberlain, who, roused by the noise, came in, in his nightcap.

"Go and drown yourself in it!" she said.

This was the last rudeness of which the princess was ever guilty; and one must allow that she had good cause to feel provoked with the lord chamberlain.

Had it been the king himself, he would have fared no better. But both he and the queen were fast asleep. And the chamberlain went back to his bed. Somehow, the doctors never came. So the princess and her old nurse were left with the prince. But the old nurse was a wise woman, and knew what to do.

They tried everything for a long time without success. The princess was nearly distracted between hope and fear, but she tried on and on, one thing after another, and everything over and over again.

At last, when they had all but given it up, just as the sun rose, the prince opened his eyes.

XV: LOOK AT THE RAIN!

HE princess burst into a passion of tears, and *fell* on the floor. There she lay for an hour, and her tears never ceased. All the pent-up crying of her life was spent now. And a rain came on, such as had never been seen in that country. The sun shone all the time, and the great drops, which fell straight to the earth, shone likewise. The palace was in the heart of a rainbow. It was a rain of rubies, and sapphires, and emeralds, and topazes. The torrents poured from the mountains like molten gold; and if it had not been for its subterraneous outlet, the lake would have overflowed and inundated the country. It was full from shore to shore.

But the princess did not heed the lake. She lay on the floor and wept. And this rain within doors was far more wonderful than the rain out of doors. For when it abated a little, and she proceeded to rise, she found, to her astonishment, that she could not. At length, after many efforts, she succeeded in getting upon her feet. But she tumbled down again directly. Hearing her fall, her old nurse uttered a yell of delight, and ran to her, screaming,—

"My darling child! she's found her gravity!"

"Oh, that's it! is it?" said the princess, rubbing her shoulder and her knee alternately. "I consider it very unpleasant. I feel as if I should be crushed to pieces."

"Hurrah!" cried the prince from the bed. "If you've come round, princess, so have I. How's the lake?"

"Brimful," answered the nurse.

"Then we're all happy."

"That we are indeed!" answered the princess, sobbing.

And there was rejoicing all over the country that rainy day. Even the babies forgot their past troubles, and danced and crowed amazingly. And the king told stories, and the queen listened to them. And he divided the money in his box, and she the honey in her pot, among all the children. And there was such jubilation as was never heard of before.

Of course the prince and princess were betrothed at once. But the princess had to learn to walk, before they could be married with any propriety. And this was not so easy at her time of life, for she could walk no more than a baby. She was always falling down and hurting herself.

"Is this the gravity you used to make so much of?" said she one day to the prince, as he raised her from the floor. "For my part, I was a great deal more comfortable without it."

"No, no, that's not it. This is it," replied the prince, as he took her up, and carried her about like a baby, kissing her all the time. "This is gravity."

"That's better," said she. "I don't mind that so much."

And she smiled the sweetest, loveliest smile in the prince's face. And she gave him one little kiss in return for all his; and he thought them overpaid, for he was beside himself with delight. I fear she complained of gravity more than once after this, notwithstanding.

It was a long time before she got reconciled to walking. But the pain of learning it was quite counterbalanced by two things, either of which would have been sufficient consolation. The first was, that the prince himself was her teacher; and the second, that she could tumble into the lake as often as she pleased. Still, she preferred to have the prince jump in with her; and the splash they made before was nothing to the splash they made now.

The lake never sank again. In process of time, it wore the roof of the cavern quite through, and was twice as deep as before.

The only revenge the princess took upon her aunt was to tread pretty hard on her gouty toe the next time she saw her. But she was sorry for it the very next day, when she heard that the water had undermined her house, and that it had fallen in the night, burying her in its ruins; whence no one ever ventured to dig up her body. There she lies to this day.

So the prince and princess lived and were happy; and had crowns of gold, and clothes of cloth, and shoes of leather, and children of boys and girls, not one of whom was ever known, on the most critical occasion, to lose the smallest atom of his or her due proportion of gravity.

THE GIANT'S HEART

THERE was once a giant who lived on the borders of Giantland where it touched on the country of common people.

Everything in Giantland was so big that the common people saw only a mass of awful mountains and clouds; and no living man had ever come from it, as far as anybody knew, to tell what he had seen in it.

Somewhere near the borders, on the other side, by the edge of a great forest, lived a labourer with his wife and a great many children. One day Tricksey-Wee, as they called her, teased her brother Buffy-Bob, till he could not bear it any longer, and gave her a box on the ear. Tricksey-Wee cried; and Buffy-Bob was so sorry and so ashamed of himself that he cried too, and ran off into the wood. He was so long gone that Tricksey-Wee began to be frightened, for she was very fond of her brother; and she was so distressed that she had first teased him and then cried, that at last she ran into the wood to look for him, though there was more chance of losing herself than of finding him. And, indeed, so it seemed likely to turn out; for, running on without looking, she at length found herself in a valley she knew nothing about. And no wonder; for what she thought was a valley with round, rocky sides, was no other than the space between

Reprinted from *Illustrated London News*, Christmas Number (1863) entitled "Tell Us a Story."

two of the roots of a great tree that grew on the borders of Giantland. She climbed over the side of it, and
went towards what she took for a black, round-topped
mountain, far away; but which she soon discovered
to be close to her, and to be a hollow place so great
that she could not tell what it was hollowed out of.
Staring at it, she found that it was a doorway; and
going nearer and staring harder, she saw the door, far
in, with a knocker of iron upon it, a great many yards
above her head, and as large as the anchor of a big
ship. Now nobody had ever been unkind to Tricksey-
Wee, and therefore she was not afraid of anybody. For
Buffy-Bob's box on the ear she did not think worth
considering. So spying a little hole at the bottom of
the door which had been nibbled by some giant
mouse, she crept through it, and found herself in an
enormous hall. She could not have seen the other
end of it at all, except for the great fire that was burning there, diminished to a spark in the distance. Towards this fire she ran as fast as she could, and was
not far from it when something fell before her with a
great clatter, over which she tumbled, and went rolling on the floor. She was not much hurt, however,
and got up in a moment. Then she saw that what she
had fallen over was not unlike a great iron bucket.
When she examined it more closely, she discovered
that it was a thimble; and looking up to see who had
dropped it, beheld a huge face, with spectacles as big
as the round windows in a church, bending over her,
and looking everywhere for the thimble. Tricksey-Wee
immediately laid hold of it in both her arms, and lifted
it about an inch nearer to the nose of the peering
giantess. This movement made the old lady see where
it was, and, her finger popping into it, it vanished
from the eyes of Tricksey-Wee, buried in the folds of
a white stocking like a cloud in the sky, which Mrs.
Giant was busy darning. For it was Saturday night,

and her husband would wear nothing but white stockings on Sunday. To be sure, he did eat little children, but only *very* little ones; and if ever it crossed his mind that it was wrong to do so, he always said to himself that he wore whiter stockings on Sunday than any other giant in all Giantland.

At the same instant Tricksey-Wee heard a sound like the wind in a tree full of leaves, and could not think what it could be; till, looking up, she found that it was the giantess whispering to her; and when she tried very hard she could hear what she said well enough.

"Run away, dear little girl," she said, "as fast as you can; for my husband will be home in a few minutes."

"But I've never been naughty to your husband," said Tricksey-Wee, looking up in the giantess's face.

"That doesn't matter. You had better go. He is fond of little children, particularly little girls."

"Oh, then he won't hurt me."

"I am not sure of that. He is so fond of them that he eats them up; and I am afraid he couldn't help hurting you a little. He's a very good man, though."

"Oh! then—" began Tricksey-Wee, feeling rather frightened; but before she could finish her sentence she heard the sound of footsteps very far apart and very heavy. The next moment, who should come running towards her, full speed, and as pale as death, but Buffy-Bob. She held out her arms, and he ran into them. But when she tried to kiss him, she only kissed the back of his head; for his white face and round eyes were turned to the door.

"Run, children; run and hide," said the giantess.

"Come, Buffy," said Tricksey; "yonder's a great brake; we'll hide in it."

The brake was a big broom; and they had just got into the bristles of it when they heard the door open with a sound of thunder, and in stalked the giant. You would have thought you saw the whole earth through the door when he opened it, so wide was it; and when he closed it, it was like nightfall.

"Where is that little boy?" he cried, with a voice like the bellowing of a cannon. "He looked a very nice boy indeed. I am almost sure he crept through the mousehole at the bottom of the door. Where is he, my dear?"

"I don't know," answered the giantess.

"But you know it is wicked to tell lies; don't you, my dear?" retorted the giant.

"Now, you ridiculous old Thunderthump!" said his wife, with a smile as broad as the sea in the sun, "how can I mend your white stockings and look after little boys? You have got plenty to last you over Sunday, I am sure. Just look what good little boys they are!"

Tricksey-Wee and Buffy-Bob peered through the bristles, and discovered a row of little boys, about a dozen, with very fat faces and goggle eyes, sitting before the fire, and looking stupidly into it. Thunderthump intended the most of these for pickling, and was feeding them well before salting them. Now and then, however, he could not keep his teeth off them, and would eat one by the bye, without salt.

He strode up to the wretched children. Now what made them very wretched indeed was, that they knew if they could only keep from eating, and grow thin, the giant would dislike them, and turn them out to find their way home; but notwithstanding this, so greedy were they, that they ate as much as ever they could hold. The giantess, who fed them, comforted herself with thinking that they were not real boys and girls, but only little pigs pretending to be boys and girls.

"Now tell me the truth," cried the giant, bending

his face down over them. They shook with terror, and every one hoped it was somebody else the giant liked best. "Where is the little boy that ran into the hall just now? Whoever tells me a lie shall be instantly boiled."

"He's in the broom," cried one dough-faced boy. "He's in there, and a little girl with him."

"The naughty children," cried the giant, "to hide from *me*!" And he made a stride towards the broom.

"Catch hold of the bristles, Bobby. Get right into a tuft, and hold on," cried Tricksey-Wee, just in time.

The giant caught up the broom, and seeing nothing under it, set it down again with a force that threw them both on the floor. He then made two strides to the boys, caught the dough-faced one by the neck, took the lid off a great pot that was boiling on the fire, popped him in as if he had been a trussed chicken, put the lid on again, and saying, "There, boys! See what comes of lying!" asked no more questions; for, as he always kept his word, he was afraid he might have to do the same to them all; and he did not like boiled boys. He liked to eat them crisp, as radishes, whether forked or not, ought to be eaten. He then sat down, and asked his wife if his supper was ready. She looked into the pot, and throwing the boy out with the ladle, as if he had been a black beetle that had tumbled in and had had the worst of it, answered that she thought it was. Whereupon he rose to help her; and taking the pot from the fire, poured the whole contents, bubbling and splashing, into a dish like a vat. Then they sat down to supper. The children in the broom could not see what they had; but it seemed to agree with them; for the giant talked like thunder, and the giantess answered like the sea, and they grew chattier and chattier. At length the giant said,—

"I don't feel quite comfortable about that heart of

The giant caught up the broom.

mine." And as he spoke, instead of laying his hand on his bosom, he waved it away towards the corner where the children were peeping from the broom bristles, like frightened little mice.

"Well, you know, my darling Thunderthump," answered his wife, "I always thought it ought to be nearer home. But you know best, of course."

"Ha! ha! You don't know where it is, wife. I moved it a month ago."

"What a man you are, Thunderthump! You trust any creature alive rather than your own wife."

Here the giantess gave a sob which sounded exactly like a wave going flop into the mouth of a cave up to the roof.

"Where have you got it now?" she resumed, checking her emotion.

"Well, Doodlem, I don't mind telling *you*," answered the giant soothingly. "The great she-eagle has got it for a nest egg. She sits on it night and day, and thinks she will bring the greatest eagle out of it that ever sharpened his beak on the rocks of Mount Sky-crack. I can warrant no one else will touch it while she has got it. But she is rather capricious, and I confess I am not easy about it; for the least scratch of one of her claws would do for me at once. And she *has* claws."

I refer any one who doubts this part of my story to certain chronicles of Giantland preserved among the Celtic nations. It was quite a common thing for a giant to put his heart out to nurse, because he did not like the trouble and responsibility of doing it himself; although I must confess it was a dangerous sort of plan to take, especially with such a delicate viscus as the heart.

All this time Buffy-Bob and Tricksey-Wee were listening with long ears.

"Oh!" thought Tricksey-Wee, "If I could but find the giant's cruel heart, wouldn't I give it a squeeze!"

The giant and giantess went on talking for a long time. The giantess kept advising the giant to hide his heart somewhere in the house; but he seemed afraid of the advantage it would give her over him.

"You could hide it at the bottom of the flour-barrel," said she.

"That would make me feel chokey," answered he.

"Well, in the coal-cellar. Or in the dust-hole—that's the place! No one would think of looking for your heart in the dust-hole."

"Worse and worse!" cried the giant.

"Well, the water-butt," suggested she.

"No, no; it would grow spongy there," said he.

"Well, what *will* you do with it?"

"I will leave it a month longer where it is, and then I will give it to the Queen of the Kangaroos, and she will carry it in her pouch for me. It is best to change its place, you know, lest my enemies should scent it out. But, dear Doodlem, it's a fretting care to have a heart of one's own to look after. The responsibility is too much for me. If it were not for a bite of a radish now and then, I never could bear it."

Here the giant looked lovingly towards the row of little boys by the fire, all of whom were nodding, or asleep on the floor.

"Why don't you trust it to me, dear Thunderthump?" said his wife. "I would take the best possible care of it."

"I don't doubt it, my love. But the responsibility would be too much for *you*. You would no longer be my darling, light-hearted, airy, laughing Doodlem. It would transform you into a heavy, oppressed woman, weary of life—as I am."

The giant closed his eyes and pretended to go to sleep. His wife got his stockings, and went on with her darning. Soon the giant's pretence became reality, and the giantess began to nod over her work.

"Now, Buffy," whispered Tricksey-Wee, "now's our time. I think it's moonlight, and we had better be off. There's a door with a hole for the cat just behind us."

"All right," said Bob; "I'm ready."

So they got out of the broom-brake and crept to the door. But to their great disappointment, when they got through it, they found themselves in a sort of shed. It was full of tubs and things, and, though it was built of wood only, they could not find a crack.

"Let us try this hole," said Tricksey; for the giant and giantess were sleeping behind them, and they dared not go back.

"All right," said Bob.

He seldom said anything else than *All right*.

Now this hole was in a mound that came in through the wall of the shed, and went along the floor for some distance. They crawled into it, and found it very dark. But groping their way along, they soon came to a small crack, through which they saw grass, pale in the moonshine. As they crept on, they found the hole began to get wider and lead upwards.

"What is that noise of rushing?" said Buffy-Bob.

"I can't tell," replied Tricksey; "for, you see, I don't know what we are in."

The fact was, they were creeping along a channel in the heart of a giant tree; and the noise they heard was the noise of the sap rushing along in its wooden pipes. When they laid their ears to the wall, they heard it gurgling along with a pleasant noise.

"It sounds kind and good," said Tricksey. "It is water running. Now it must be running from some-where to somewhere. I think we had better go on, and we shall come somewhere."

It was now rather difficult to go on, for they had

to climb as if they were climbing a hill; and now the passage was wide. Nearly worn out, they saw light overhead at last, and creeping through a crack into the open air, found themselves on the fork of a huge tree. A great, broad, uneven space lay around them, out of which spread boughs in every direction, the smallest of them as big as the biggest tree in the country of common people. Overhead were leaves enough to supply all the trees they had ever seen. Not much moonlight could come through, but the leaves would glimmer white in the wind at times. The tree was full of giant birds. Every now and then, one would sweep through, with a great noise. But, except an occasional chirp, sounding like a shrill pipe in a great organ, they made no noise. All at once an owl began to hoot. He thought he was singing. As soon as he began, other birds replied, making rare game of him. To their astonishment, the children found they could understand every word they sang. And what they sang was something like this:—

"I will sing a song.
I'm the owl."
"Sing a song, you sing-song
Ugly fowl!
What will you sing about,
Night in and Day out?"

"Sing about the night;
I'm the owl."
"You could not see for the light,
Stupid fowl!"
"Oh! the moon! and the dew!
And the shadows! —tu-whoo!"

63

The owl spread out his silent, soft, sly wings, and lighting between Tricksey-Wee and Buffy-Bob, nearly smothered them, closing up one under each wing. It was like being buried in a down bed. But the owl did not like anything between his sides and his wings, so he opened his wings again, and the children made haste to get out. Tricksey-Wee immediately went in front of the bird, and looking up into his huge face, which was as round as the eyes of the giantess's spectacles, and much bigger, dropped a pretty curtsy, and said,—

"Please, Mr. Owl, I want to whisper to you."

"Very well, small child," answered the owl, looking important, and stooping his ear towards her. "What is it?"

"Please tell me where the eagle lives that sits on the giant's heart."

"Oh, you naughty child! That's a secret. For shame!"

And with a great hiss that terrified them, the owl flew into the tree. All birds are fond of secrets; but not many of them can keep them so well as the owl.

So the children went on because they did not know what else to do. They found the way very rough and difficult, the tree was so full of humps and hollows. Now and then they plashed into a pool of rain; now and then they came upon twigs growing out of the trunk where they had no business, and they were as large as full-grown poplars. Sometimes they came upon great cushions of soft moss, and on one of them they lay down and rested. But they had not lain long before they spied a large nightingale sitting on a branch, with its bright eyes looking up at the moon. In a moment more he began to sing, and the birds about him began to reply, but in a very different tone from that in which they had replied to the owl. Oh, the birds did call the nightingale such pretty names!

The nightingale sang, and the birds replied like this:—

> "I will sing a song.
>   I'm the nightingale."
> "Sing a song, long, long,
>   Little Neverfail!
> What will you sing about,
> Light in or light out?"

> "Sing about the light
>   Gone away;
> Down, away, and out of sight —
>   Poor lost day!
> Mourning for the day dead,
> O'er his dim bed."

The nightingale sang so sweetly, that the children would have fallen asleep but for fear of losing any of the song. When the nightingale stopped they got up and wandered on. They did not know where they were going, but they thought it best to keep going on, because then they might come upon something or other. They were very sorry they had forgotten to ask the nightingale about the eagle's nest, but his music had put everything else out of their heads. They resolved, however, not to forget the next time they had a chance. So they went on and on, till they were both tired, and Tricksey-Wee said at last, trying to laugh,—

"I declare my legs feel just like a Dutch doll's."

"Then here's the place to go to bed in," said Buffy-Bob.

They stood at the edge of a last year's nest, and looked down with delight into the round, mossy cave. Then they crept gently in, and lying down in each other's arms, found it so deep, and warm, and comfortable, and soft, that they were soon fast asleep.

Now close beside them, in a hollow, was another nest, in which lay a lark and his wife; and the children were awakened, very early in the morning, by a dispute between Mr. and Mrs. Lark.

"Let me up," said the lark.

"It is not time," said the lark's wife.

"It is," said the lark, rather rudely. "The darkness is quite thin. I can almost see my own beak."

"Nonsense!" said the lark's wife. "You know you came home yesterday morning quite worn out—you had to fly so very high before you saw him. I am sure he would not mind if you took it a little easier. Do be quiet and go to sleep again."

"That's not it at all," said the lark. "He doesn't want me. I want him. Let me up, I say."

He began to sing; and Tricksey-Wee and Buffy-Bob, having now learned the way, answered him:—

> *"I will sing a song,*
> *I'm the Lark."*
> *"Sing, sing, Throat-strong,*
> *Little Kill-the-dark.*
> *What will you sing about,*
> *Now the night is out?"*

> *"I can only call,*
> *I can't think.*
> *Let me up—that's all.*
> *Let me drink!*
> *Thirsting all the long night*
> *For a drink of light."*

By this time the lark was standing on the edge of his nest and looking at the children.

"Poor little things! You can't fly," said the lark.

"No; but we can look up," said Tricksey.

"Ah, you don't know what it is to see the very first of the sun."

"But we know what it is to wait till he comes. He's no worse for your seeing him first, is he?"

"Oh no, certainly not," answered the lark, with condescension; and then, bursting into his *Jubilate*, he sprang aloft, clapping his wings like a clock running down.

"Tell us where—" began Buffy-Bob.

But the lark was out of sight. His song was all that was left of him. That was everywhere, and he was nowhere.

"Selfish bird!" said Buffy. "It's all very well for larks to go hunting the sun, but they have no business to despise their neighbors, for all that."

"Can I be of any use to you?" said a sweet birdvoice out of the nest.

This was the lark's wife, who stayed at home with the young larks while her husband went to church.

"Oh! thank you. If you please," answered Tricksey-Wee.

And up popped a pretty brown head; and then up came a brown feathery body; and last of all came the slender legs on to the edge of the nest. There she turned, and, looking down into the nest, from which came a whole litany of chirpings for breakfast, said, "Lie still, little ones." Then she turned to the children.

"My husband is King of the Larks," she said.

Buffy-Bob took off his cap, and Tricksey-Wee curtsied very low.

"Oh, it's not me," said the bird, looking very shy. "I am only his wife. It's my husband."

And she looked up after him into the sky, whence his song was still falling like a shower of musical hailstones. Perhaps *she* could see him.

"He's a splendid bird," said Buffy-Bob; "only you know he *will* get up a little too early."

"Oh, no! he doesn't. It's only his way, you know. But tell me what I can do for you."

"Tell us, please, Lady Lark, where the she-eagle lives that sits on Giant Thunderthump's heart."

"Oh! that is a secret."

"Did you promise not to tell?"

"No; but larks ought to be discreet. They see more than other birds."

"But you don't fly up high like your husband, do you?"

"Not often. But it's no matter. I come to know things for all that."

"Do tell me, and I will sing you a song," said Tricksey-Wee.

"Can you sing too?—You have got no wings!"

"Yes. And I will sing you a song I learned the other day about a lark and his wife."

"Please do," said the lark's wife. "Be quiet, children, and listen."

Tricksey-Wee was very glad she happened to know a song which would please the lark's wife, at least, whatever the lark himself might have thought of it, if he had heard it. So she sang:—

" 'Good-morrow, my lord!' in the sky alone,
Sang the lark, as the sun ascended his throne.
'Shine on me, my lord; I only am come,
Of all your servants, to welcome you home.
I have flown a whole hour, right up, I swear,
To catch the first shine of your golden hair!'

" 'Must I thank you, then,' said the king, 'Sir Lark,
For flying so high, and hating the dark?
You ask a full cup for half a thirst:

Half is love of me, and half love to be first.
There's many a bird that makes no haste,
But waits till I come. That's as much to my taste.'

"And the king hid his head in a turban of cloud,
And the lark stopped singing, quite vexed and cowed.
But he flew up higher, and thought, 'Anon,
The wrath of the king will be over and gone,
And his crown, shining out of its cloudy fold,
Will change my brown feathers to a glory of gold.'

"So he flew, with the strength of a lark he flew.
But as he rose the cloud rose too,
And not a gleam of the golden hair
Came through the depth of the misty air,
Till, weary with flying, with sighing sore,
The strong sun-seeker could do no more.

"His wings had had no chrism of gold,
And his feathers felt withered and worn and old,
So he quivered and sank, and dropped like a stone.
And there on his nest, where he left her, alone,
Sat his little wife on her little eggs,
Keeping them warm with wings and legs.

"Did I say alone? Ah, no such thing!
Full in her face was shining the king.
'Welcome, Sir Lark! You look tired,' said he.
'Up is not always the best way to me.
While you have been singing so high and away,
I've been shining to your little wife all day.'

"He had set his crown all about the nest,
And out of the midst shone her little brown breast;
And so glorious was she in russet gold,
That for wonder and awe Sir Lark grew cold.
He popped his head under her wing, and lay
As still as a stone, till the king was away."

As soon as Tricksey-Wee had finished her song, the lark's wife began a low, sweet, modest little song of her own; and after she had piped away for two or three minutes, she said,—

"You dear children, what can I do for you?"

"Tell us where the she-eagle lives, please," said Tricksey-Wee.

"Well, I don't think there can be much harm in telling such wise, good children," said Lady Lark; "I am sure you don't want to do any mischief."

"Oh, no; quite the contrary," said Buffy-Bob.

"Then I'll tell you. She lives on the very topmost peak of Mount Skycrack; and the only way to get up is to climb on the spiders' webs that cover it from top to bottom."

"That's rather serious," said Tricksey-Wee.

"But you don't want to go up, you foolish little thing! You can't go. And what do you want to go up for?"

"That is a secret," said Tricksey-Wee.

"Well, it's no business of mine," rejoined Lady Lark, a little offended, and quite vexed that she had told them. So she flew away to find some breakfast for her little ones, who by this time were chirping very impatiently. The children looked at each other, joined hands, and walked off.

In a minute more the sun was up, and they soon reached the outside of the tree. The bark was so knobby and rough, and full of twigs, that they managed to get down, though not without great difficulty. Then, far away to the north they saw a huge peak, like the spire of a church, going right up into the sky. They thought this must be Mount Skycrack, and turned their faces towards it. As they went on, they saw a giant or two, now and then, striding about the fields or through the woods, but they kept out of their way. Nor were they in much danger; for it was only one or two of the border giants that were so very fond of children.

At last they came to the foot of Mount Skycrack. It stood in a plain alone, and shot right up, I don't know how many thousand feet, into the air, a long, narrow, spearlike mountain. The whole face of it, from top to bottom, was covered with a network of spiders' webs, the threads of various sizes, from that of silk to that of whipcord. The webs shook, and quivered, and waved in the sun, glittering like silver. All about ran huge greedy spiders, catching huge silly flies, and devouring them.

Here they sat down to consider what could be done. The spiders did not heed them, but ate away at the flies. —Now at the foot of the mountain, and all round it, was a ring of water, not very broad, but very deep. As they sat watching them, one of the spiders, whose web was woven across this water, somehow or other lost his hold, and fell in on his back. Tricksey-Wee and Buffy-Bob ran to his assistance, and laying hold each of one of his legs, succeeded, with the help of the other legs, which struggled spiderfully, in getting him out upon dry land. As soon as he had shaken himself, and dried himself a little, the spider turned to the children, saying, —

"And now, what can I do for you?"

"Tell us, please," said they, "how we can get up the mountain to the she-eagle's nest."

"Nothing is easier," answered the spider. "Just run

up there, and tell them all I sent you, and nobody will mind you."

"But we haven't got claws like you, Mr. Spider," said Buffy.

"Ah! no more you have, poor unprovided creatures! Still, I think we can manage it. Come home with me."

"You won't eat us, will you?" said Buffy.

"My dear child," answered the spider, in a tone of injured dignity, "I eat nothing but what is mischievous or useless. You have helped me, and now I will help you."

The children rose at once, and climbing as well as they could, reached the spider's nest in the centre of the web. Nor did they find it very difficult; for whenever too great a gap came, the spider spinning a strong cord stretched it just where they would have chosen to put their feet next. He left them in his nest, after bringing them two enormous honey-bags, taken from bees that he had caught but presently about six of the wisest of the spiders came back with him. It was horrible to look up and see them all round the mouth of the nest, looking down on them in contemplation, as if wondering whether they would be nice eating. At length one of them said,—"Tell us truly what you want with the eagle, and we will try to help you."

Then Tricksey-Wee told them that there was a giant on the borders who treated little children no better than radishes, and that they had narrowly escaped being eaten by him; that they had found out that the great she-eagle of Mount Skycrack was at present sitting on his heart; and that, if they could only get hold of his heart, they would soon teach the giant better behaviour.

"But," said their host, "if you get at the heart of the giant, you will find it as large as one of your elephants. What can you do with it?"

"The least scratch will kill it," replied Buffy-Bob.

"Ah! but you might do better than that," said the spider. —"Now we have resolved to help you. Here is a little bag of spider-juice. The giants cannot bear spiders, and this juice is dreadful poison to them. We are all ready to go up with you, and drive the eagle away. Then you must put the heart into this other bag, and bring it down with you; for then the giant will be in your power."

"But how can we do that?" said Buffy. "The bag is not much bigger than a pudding-bag."

"But it is as large as you will be able to carry."

"Yes; but what are we to do with the heart?"

"Put it into the bag, to be sure. Only, first, you must squeeze out a drop of the other bag upon it. You will see what will happen."

"Very well; we will do as you tell us," said Tricksey-Wee. "And now, if you please, how shall we go?"

"Oh, that's our business," said the first spider. "You come with me, and my grandfather will take your brother. Get up."

So Tricksey-Wee mounted on the narrow part of the spider's back, and held fast. And Buffy-Bob got on the grandfather's back. And up they scrambled, over one web after another, up and up—so fast! And every spider followed; so that, when Tricksey-Wee looked back, she saw a whole army of spiders scrambling after them.

"What can we want with so many?" she thought; but she said nothing.

The moon was now up, and it was a splendid sight below and around them. All Giantland was spread out under them, with its great hills, lakes, trees, and animals. And all above them was the clear heaven, and Mount Skycrack rising into it, with its endless ladders of spiderwebs, glittering like cords made of moonbeams. And up the moonbeams went, crawling and scrambling, and racing, a huge army of spiders.

At length they reached all but the very summit, where they stopped. Tricksey-Wee and Buffy-Bob could see above them a great globe of feathers, that finished off the mountain like an ornamental knob.

"But how shall we drive her off?" said Buffy.

"We'll soon manage that," answered the grandfather-spider. "Come on you, down there."

Up rushed the whole army, past the children, over the edge of the nest, on to the she-eagle, and buried themselves in her feathers. In a moment she became very restless, and went pecking about with her beak.

All at once she spread out her wings, with a sound like a whirlwind, and flew off to bathe in the sea; and then the spiders began to drop from her in all directions on their gossamer wings. The children had to hold fast to keep the wind of the eagle's flight from blowing them off. As soon as it was over, they looked into the nest, and there lay the giant's heart—an awful and ugly thing.

"Make haste, child!" said Tricksey's spider.

So Tricksey took her bag, and squeezed a drop out of it upon the heart. She thought she heard the giant give a far-off roar of pain, and she nearly fell from her seat with terror. The heart instantly began to shrink. It shrank and shrivelled till it was nearly gone; and Buffy-Bob caught it up and put it into his bag. Then the two spiders turned and went down again as fast as they could. Before they got to the bottom, they heard the shrieks of the she-eagle over the loss of her egg; but the spiders told them not to be alarmed, for her eyes were too big to see them.—By the time they reached the foot of the mountain, all the spiders had got home, and were busy again catching flies, as if nothing had happened.

After renewed thanks to their friends, the children set off, carrying the giant's heart with them.

"If you should find it at all troublesome, just give it a little more spider-juice directly," said the grandfather, as they took their leave.

Now the giant had given an awful roar of pain the moment they anointed his heart, and had fallen down in a fit, in which he lay so long that all the boys might have escaped if they had not been so fat. One did, and got home in safety. For days the giant was unable to speak. The first words he uttered were,—

"Oh, my heart! my heart!"

"Your heart is safe enough, dear Thunderthump,"

said his wife. "Really, a man of your size ought not to be so nervous and apprehensive. I am ashamed of you."

"You have no heart, Doodlem," answered he. "I assure you that at this moment mine is in the greatest danger. It has fallen into the hands of foes, though who they are I cannot tell."

Here he fainted again; for Tricksey-Wee, finding the heart beginning to swell a little, had given it the least touch of spider-juice.

Again he recovered, and said,—

"Dear Doodlem, my heart is coming back to me. It is coming nearer and nearer."

After lying silent for hours, he exclaimed,—

"It is in the house, I know!"

And he jumped up and walked about, looking in every corner.

As he rose, Tricksey-Wee and Buffy-Bob came out of the hole in the tree-root, and through the cat-hole in the door, and walked boldly towards the giant. Both kept their eyes busy watching him. Led by the love of his own heart, the giant soon spied them, and staggered furiously towards them.

"I will eat you, you vermin!" he cried. "Here with my heart!"

Tricksey gave the heart a sharp pinch. Down fell the giant on his knees, blubbering, and crying, and begging for his heart.

"You shall have it, if you behave yourself properly," said Tricksey.

"How shall I behave myself properly?" asked he, whimpering.

"Take all those boys and girls, and carry them home at once."

"I'm not able; I'm too ill. I should fall down."

"Take them up directly."

"I can't, till you give me my heart."

"Very well!" said Tricksey; and she gave the heart another pinch.

The giant jumped to his feet, and catching up all the children, thrust some into his waistcoat-pockets, some into his breast-pocket, put two or three into his hat, and took a bundle of them under each arm. Then he staggered to the door.

All this time poor Doodlem was sitting in her arm-chair, crying, and mending a white stocking.

The giant led the way to the borders. He could not go fast but that Buffy and Tricksey managed to keep up with him. When they reached the borders, they thought it would be safer to let the children find their own way home. So they told him to set them down. He obeyed.

"Have you put them all down, Mr. Thunder-thump?" asked Tricksey-Wee.

"Yes," said the giant.

"That's a lie!" squeaked a little voice; and out came a head from his waistcoat pocket.

Tricksey-Wee pinched the heart till the giant roared with pain.

"You're not a gentleman. You tell stories," she said.

"He was the thinnest of the lot," said Thunder-thump, crying.

"Are you all there now, children?" asked Tricksey.

"Yes, ma'am," returned they, after counting them-selves very carefully, and with some difficulty; for they were all stupid children.

"Now," said Tricksey-Wee to the giant, "will you promise to carry off no more children, and never to eat a child again all your life?"

"Yes, yes! I promise," answered Thunderthump, sobbing.

"And you will never cross the borders of Giant-land?"

77

"Never."

"And you shall never again wear white stockings on a Sunday, all your life long.—Do you promise?"

The giant hesitated at this, and began to expostulate; but Tricksey-Wee, believing it would be good for his morals, insisted; and the giant promised.

Then she required of him, that, when she gave him back his heart, he should give it to his wife to take care of for him for ever after. The poor giant fell on his knees, and began again to beg. But Tricksey-Wee giving the heart a slight pinch, he bawled out,—

"Yes, yes! Doodlem shall have it, I swear. Only she must not put it in the flour barrel, or in the dusthole."

"Certainly not. Make your own bargain with her.—And you promise not to interfere with my brother and me, or to take any revenge for what we have done?"

"Yes, yes, my dear children; I promise everything. Do, pray, make haste and give me back my poor heart."

"Wait there, then, till I bring it to you."

"Yes, yes. Only make haste, for I feel very faint."

Tricksey-Wee began to undo the mouth of the bag. But Buffy-Bob, who had got very knowing on his travels, took out his knife with the pretence of cutting the string; but, in reality, to be prepared for any emergency.

No sooner was the heart out of the bag, than it expanded to the size of a bullock; and the giant, with a yell of rage and vengeance, rushed on the two children, who had stepped sideways from the terrible heart. But Buffy-Bob was too quick for Thunderthump. He sprang to the heart, and buried his knife in it, up to the hilt. A fountain of blood spouted from it; and with a dreadful groan the giant fell dead at the feet of little Tricksey-Wee, who could not help being sorry for him, after all.

THE CARASOYN

I: THE MOUNTAIN STREAM

ONCE upon a time, there lived in a valley in Scotland, a boy about twelve years of age, the son of a shepherd. His mother was dead, and he had no sister or brother. His father was out all day on the hills with his sheep; but when he came home at night, he was as sure of finding the cottage neat and clean, the floor swept, a bright fire, and his supper waiting for him, as if he had had wife and daughter to look after his household, instead of only a boy. Therefore, although Colin could only read and write, and knew nothing of figures, he was ten times wiser, and more capable of learning anything, than if he had been at school all his days. He was never at a loss when anything had to be done. Somehow, he always blundered into the straight road to his end, while another would be putting on his shoes to look for it. And yet all the time that he was busiest working, he was busiest building castles in the air. I think the two ought always to go together.

And so Colin was never over-worked, but had plenty of time to himself. In winter he spent it in reading by the fireside, or carving pieces of wood with his pocket knife; and in summer he always went out for a ramble. His great delight was in a little stream

The first part appeared as "The Fairy Fleet" in *Argosy* (1866); the expanded form "The Carasoyn" appeared in *Works* (1871).

which ran down the valley from the mountains above. Up this *burn* he would wander every afternoon, with his hands in his pockets. He never got far, however—he was so absorbed in watching its antics. Sometimes he would sit on a rock, staring at the water as it hurried through the stones, scolding, expostulating, muttering, and always having its own way. Sometimes he would stop by a deep pool, and watch the crimson-spotted trouts, darting about as if their thoughts and not their tails sent them where they wanted to go. And when he stopped at the little cascade, tumbling smooth and shining over a hollowed rock, he seldom got beyond it.

But there was one thing which always troubled him. It was, that when the stream came near the cottage, it could find no other way than through the little yard where stood the cowhouse and the pigsty; and there, not finding a suitable channel, spread abroad in a disconsolate manner, becoming rather a puddle than a brook, all defiled with the treading of the cloven feet of the cow and the pigs. In fact, it looked quite lost and ruined; so that even after it had, with much labour, got out of the yard again, it took a long time to gather itself together, and not quite succeeding, slipped away as if ashamed, with spent forces and poverty-stricken speed; till at length, meeting the friendly help of a rivulet coming straight from the hills, it gathered heart and bounded on afresh.

"It can't be all that the cow drinks that makes the difference," said Colin to himself. "The pigs don't care about it. I do believe it's affronted at being dashed about. The cow isn't dirty, but she's rather stupid and inconsiderate. The pigs are dirty. Something must be done. Let me see."

He reconnoitred the whole ground. Upon the other side of the house all was rock, through which he

could not cut; and he was forced to the conclusion
that the only other course for the stream to take lay
right through the cottage.

To most engineers this would have appeared the
one course to be avoided; but Colin's heart danced at
the thought of having his dear *burn* running right
through the house. How cool it would be all the summer! How convenient for cooking; and how handy at
meals! And then the music of it! How it would tell
him stories, and sing him to sleep at night! What a
companion it would be when his father was away!
And then he could bathe in it when he liked. In winter—ah!—to be sure! But winter was a long way off.

The very next day his father went to the fair. So
Colin set to work at once.

It was not such a very difficult undertaking; for the
walls of the cottage, and the floor as well, were of
clay—the former nearly sun-dried into a brick, and
the latter trampled hard; but still both assailable by
pickaxe and spade. He cut through the walls, and
dug a channel along the floor, letting in stones in the
bottom and sides. After it got out of the cottage and
through the small garden in front, it should find its
own way to the channel below, for here the hill was
very steep.

The same evening his father came home.

"What have you been about, Colin?" he asked, in
great surprise, when he saw the trench in the floor.

"Wait a minute, father," said Colin, "till I have got
your supper, and then I'll tell you."

So when his father was seated at the table, Colin
darted out, and hurrying up to the stream, broke
through the bank just in the place whence a natural
hollow led straight to the cottage. The stream dashed
out like a wild creature from a cage, faster than he
could follow, and shot through the wall of the cottage.
His father gave a shout; and when Colin went in, he

found him sitting with his spoon half-way to his mouth, and his eyes fixed on the muddy water which rushed foaming through his floor.

"It will soon be clean, father," said Colin, "and then it will be so nice!"

His father made no answer, but continued staring. Colin went on with a long list of the advantages of having a brook running through your house. At length his father smiled and said:—

"You are a curious creature, Colin. But why shouldn't you have your fancies as well as older people? We'll try it awhile, and then we'll see about it."

The fact was, Colin's father had often thought what a lonely life the boy's was. And it seemed hard to take from him any pleasure he could have. So out rushed Colin at the front, to see how the brook would take the shortest way headlong down the hill to its old channel. And to see it go tumbling down that hill was a sight worth living for.

"It is a mercy," said Colin, "it has no neck to break, or it would break twenty times in a minute. It flings itself from rock to rock right down, just as I should like to do, if it weren't for my neck."

All that evening he was out and in without a moment's rest; now up to the beginning of the cut, now following the stream down to the cottage; then through the cottage, and out again at the front door to see it dart across the garden, and dash itself down the hill.

At length his father told him he must go to bed. He took one more peep at the water, which was running quite clear now, and obeyed. His father followed him presently.

II: THE FAIRY FLEET

THE bed was about a couple of yards from the edge of the brook. And as Colin was always first

up in the morning, he slept at the front of the bed.
So he lay for some time gazing at the faint glimmer
of the water in the dull red light from the sod-covered
fire, and listening to its sweet music as it hurried
through to the night again, till its murmur changed
into a lullaby, and sung him fast asleep.

Soon he found that he was coming awake again.
He was lying listening to the sound of the busy
stream. But it had gathered more sounds since he
went to sleep—amongst the rest, one of boards
knocking together, and a tiny chattering and sweet
laughter, like the tinkling of heather-bells. He opened
his eyes. The moon was shining along the brook,
lighting the smoky rafters above with its reflection
from the water, which had been dammed back at its
outlet from the cottage, so that it lay bank-full and
level with the floor. But its surface was hardly to be
seen, save by an occasional glimmer, for the crowded
boats of a fairy fleet which had just arrived. The sailors were as busy as sailors could be, mooring along
the banks, or running their boats high and dry on the
shore. Some had little sails which glimmered white
in the moonshine—half-lowered, or blowing out in
the light breeze that crept down the course of the
stream. Some were pulling about through the rest,
oars flashing, tiny voices calling, tiny feet running,
tiny hands hauling at ropes that ran through blocks
of shining ivory. On the shore stood groups of fairy
ladies in all colours of the rainbow, green predomi-
nating, waited upon by gentlemen all in green, but
with red and yellow feathers in their caps. The queen
had landed on the side next to Colin, and in a few
minutes more twenty dances were going at once along
the shores of the fairy river. And there lay great Colin's
face, just above the bed-clothes, *glowering* at them
like an ogre.

At last, after a few dances, he heard a clear, sweet, ringing voice say,

"I've had enough of this. I'm tired of doing like the big people. Let's have a game of Hey Cockolorum Jig!"

That instant every group sprang asunder, and every fairy began a frolic on his own account. They scattered all over the cottage, and Colin lost sight of most of them.

While he lay watching the antics of two of those near him, who behaved more like clowns at a fair than the gentlemen they had been a little while before, he heard a voice close to his ear; but though he looked everywhere about his pillow, he could see nothing. The voice stopped the moment he began to look, but began again as soon as he gave it up.

"You can't see me. I'm talking to you through a hole in the head of your bed."

"Don't look," said the voice. "If the queen sees me I shall be pinched. Oh, please don't."

The voice sounded as if its owner would cry presently. So Colin took good care not to look. It went on:

"Please, I am a little girl, not a fairy. The queen stole me the minute I was born, seven years ago, and I can't get away. I don't like the fairies. They are so silly. And they never grow any wiser. I grow wiser every year. I want to get back to my own people. They won't let me. They make me play at being somebody else all night long, and sleep all day. That's what they do themselves. And I should so like to be myself. The queen says that's not the way to be happy at all; but I do want very much to be a little girl. Do take me."

"How am I to get you?" asked Colin in a whisper, which sounded, after the sweet voice of the changeling, like the wind in a field of dry beans.

"The queen is so pleased with you that she is sure to offer you something. Choose me. Here she comes."

Immediately he heard another voice, shriller and stronger, in front of him; and, looking about, saw standing on the edge of the bed a lovely little creature, with a crown glittering with jewels, and a rush for a sceptre in her hand, the blossom of which shone like a bunch of garnets.

"You great staring creature!" she said. "Your eyes are much too big to see with. What clumsy hobgoblins you thick folk are!"

So saying, she laid her wand across Colin's eyes.

"Now, then, stupid!" she said and that instant Colin saw the room like a huge barn, full of creatures about two feet high. The beams overhead were crowded with fairies, playing all imaginable tricks, scrambling everywhere, knocking each other over, throwing dust and soot in each other's faces, grinning from behind corners, dropping on each other's necks, and tripping up each other's heels. Two had got hold of an empty egg-shell, and coming behind one sitting on the edge of the table, and laughing at some one on the floor, tumbled it right over him, so that he was lost in the cavernous hollow. But the lady-fairies mingled in none of these rough pranks. Their tricks were always graceful, and they had more to say than to do.

But the moment the queen had laid her wand across his eyes, she went on:

"Know, son of a human mortal, that thou hast pleased a queen of the fairies. Lady as I am over the elements, I cannot have everything I desire. One thing thou hast given me. Years have I longed for a path down this rivulet to the ocean below. Your horrid farm-yard, ever since your great-grandfather built this cottage, was the one obstacle. For we fairies hate dirt, not only in houses, but in fields and woods as well, and above all in running streams. But I can't talk like

Colin saw standing on the edge of the bed
a lovely little creature.

this any longer. I tell you what, you are a dear good boy, and you shall have what you please. Ask me for anything you like."

"May it please your majesty," said Colin, very deliberately, "I want a little girl that you carried away some seven years ago the moment she was born. May it please your majesty, I want her."

"It does not please my majesty," cried the queen, whose face had been growing very black. "Ask for something else."

"Then, whether it pleases your majesty or not," said Colin, bravely, "I hold your majesty to your word. I want that little girl, and that little girl I *will* have, and nothing else."

"You dare to talk so to me, you thick!"

"Yes, your majesty."

"Then you sha'n't have her."

"Then I'll turn the brook right through the dunghill," said Colin. "Do you think I'll let you come into my cottage to play at high jinks when you please, if you behave to me like this?"

And Colin sat up in bed, and looked the queen in the face. And as he did so he caught sight of the loveliest little creature peeping round the corner at the foot of the bed. And he knew she was the little girl because she was quiet, and looked frightened, and was sucking her thumb.

Then the queen, seeing with whom she had to deal, and knowing that queens in Fairyland are bound by their word, began to try another plan with him. She put on her sweetest manner and looks; and as she did so, the little face at the foot of the bed grew more troubled, and the little head shook itself, and the little thumb dropped out of the little mouth.

"Dear Colin," said the queen, "you shall have the girl. But you must do something for me first."

The little girl shook her head as fast as ever she could, but Colin was taken up with the queen.

"To be sure I will. What is it?" he said.

And so he was bound by a new bargain, and was in the queen's power.

"You must fetch me a bottle of Carasoyn," said she.

"What is that?" asked Colin.

"A kind of wine that makes people happy."

"Why, are you not happy already?"

"No, Colin," answered the queen, with a sigh.

"You have everything you want."

"Except the Carasoyn," returned the queen.

"You do whatever you like, and go wherever you please."

"That's just it. I want something that I neither like nor please—that I don't know anything about. I want a bottle of Carasoyn."

And here she cried like a spoilt child, not like a sorrowful woman.

"But how am I to get it?"

"I don't know. You must find out."

"Oh! that's not fair," cried Colin.

But the queen burst into a fit of laughter that sounded like the bells of a hundred frolicking sheep, and bounding away to the side of the river, jumped on board of her boat. And like a swarm of bees gathered the courtiers and sailors; two creeping out of the bellows, one at the nozzle and the other at the valve; three out of the basket-hilt of the broadsword on the wall; six all white out of the meal-tub; and so from all parts of the cottage to the river-side. And amongst them Colin spied the little girl creeping on board the queen's boat, with her pinafore to her eyes; and the queen was shaking her fist at her. In five minutes more they had all scrambled into the boats, and the whole fleet was in motion down the stream. In another moment the cottage was empty, and everything had returned to its usual size.

"They'll be all dashed to pieces on the rocks," cried Colin, jumping up, and running into the garden. When he reached the fall, there was nothing to be seen but the swift plunge and rush of the broken water in the moonlight. He thought he heard cries and shouts coming up from below, and fancied he could distinguish the sobs of the little maiden whom he had so foolishly lost. But the sounds might be only those of the water, for to the different voices of a running stream there is no end. He followed its course all the way to its old channel, but saw nothing to indicate any disaster. Then he crept back to his bed, where he lay thinking what a fool he had been, till he cried himself to sleep over the little girl who would never grow into a woman.

III: THE OLD WOMAN AND HER HEN

IN the morning, however, his courage had returned; for the word Carasoyn was always saying itself in his brain.

"People in fairy stories," he said, "always find what they want. Why should not I find this Carasoyn? It does not seem likely. But the world doesn't go round by *likely*. So I will try."

But how was he to begin?

When Colin did not know what to do, he always did something. So as soon as his father was gone to the hill, he wandered up the stream down which the fairies had come.

"But I needn't go on so," he said, "for if the Carasoyn grew in the fairies' country, the queen would know how to get it."

All at once he remembered how he had lost himself on the moor when he was a little boy; and had gone into a hut and found there an old woman spinning. And she had told him such stories! and shown him the way home. So he thought she might be able to help him now; for he remembered that she was very old then, and must be older and still wiser now. And he resolved to go and look for the hut, and ask the old woman what he was to do.

So he left the stream, and climbed the hill, and soon came upon a desolate moor. The sun was clouded and the wind was cold, and everything looked dreary. And there was no sign of a hut anywhere. He wandered on, looking for it; and all at once found that he had forgotten the way back. At the same instant he saw the hut right before him. And then he remembered it was when he had lost himself that he saw it the former time.

"It seems the way to find some things is to lose yourself," said he to himself.

He went up to the cottage, which was like a large beehive built of turf, and knocked at the door.

"Come in, Colin," said a voice; and he entered, stooping low.

The old woman sat by a little fire, spinning, after the old fashion, with a distaff and spindle. She stopped the moment he went in.

"Come and sit down by the fire," she said, "and tell me what you want."

Then Colin saw that she had no eyes.

"I am very sorry you are blind," he said.

"Never you mind that, my dear. I see more than you do for all my blindness. Tell me what you want, and I shall see at least what I can do for you."

"How do you know I want anything?" asked Colin.

"Now that's what I don't like," said the old woman. "Why do you waste words? Words should not be wasted any more than crumbs."

"I beg your pardon," returned Colin. "I will tell you all about it."

And so he told her the whole story.

"Oh those children! those children!" said the old woman. "They are always doing some mischief. They never know how to enjoy themselves without hurting somebody or other. I really must give that queen a bit of my mind. Well, my dear, I like you; and I will tell you what must be done. You shall carry the silly queen her bottle of Carasoyn. But she won't like it when she gets it, I can tell her. That's my business, however.—First of all, Colin, you must dream three days without sleeping. Next, you must work three days without dreaming. And last, you must work and dream three days together."

"How am I to do all that?"

"I will help you all I can, but a great deal will depend on yourself. In the meantime you must have something to eat.

So saying, she rose, and going to a corner behind her bed, returned with a large golden-coloured egg in her hand. This she laid on the hearth, and covered over with hot ashes. She then chatted away to Colin about his father, and the sheep, and the cow, and the housework, and showed that she knew all about him. At length she drew the ashes off the egg, and put it on the plate.

"It shines like silver now," said Colin.

"That is a sign it is quite done," said she, and set it before him.

Colin had never tasted anything half so nice. And he had never seen such a quantity of meat in an egg. Before he had finished it he had made a hearty meal. But, in the meantime, the old woman said,—

"Shall I tell you a story while you have your dinner?"

"Oh, yes, please do," answered Colin. "You told me such stories before!"

"Jenny," said the old woman, "my wool is all done. Get me some more."

And from behind the bed out came a sober-coloured, but large and beautifully-shaped hen. She walked sedately across the floor, putting down her feet daintily, like a prim matron as she was, and stopping by the door, gave a *cluck, cluck*.

"Oh, the door is shut, is it?" said the old woman.

"Let me open it," said Colin.

"Do, my dear."

"What are all those white things?" he asked, for the cottage stood in the middle of a great bed of grass with white tops.

"Those are my sheep," said the old woman. "You will see."

Into the grass Jenny walked, and stretching up her neck, gathered the white woolly stuff in her beak. When she had as much as she could hold, she came back and dropped it on the floor; then picked the seeds out and swallowed them, and went back for more. The old woman took the wool, and fastening it on her distaff, began to spin, giving the spindle a twirl, and then dropping it and drawing out the thread from the distaff. But as soon as the spindle began to twirl, it began to sparkle all the colours of the rainbow, that it was a delight to see. And the hands of the woman, instead of being old and wrinkled, were young and long-fingered and fair, and they drew out the wool, and the spindle spun and flashed, and the hen kept going out and in, bringing wool and swallowing the seeds, and the old woman kept telling Colin one story after another, till he thought he could sit there all his life and listen. Sometimes it seemed the spindle that was flashing them, sometimes the long fingers that were spinning them, and sometimes the hen that was gathering them off the roads of the long dry grass and bringing them in her beak and laying them down on the floor.

All at once the spindle grew slower, and gradually ceased turning; the fingers stopped drawing out the thread, the hen retreated behind the bed, and the voice of the blind woman was silent.

"I suppose it is time for me to go," said Colin.

"Yes, it is," answered his hostess.

"Please tell me, then, how I am to dream three days without sleeping."

"That's over," said the old woman. "You've just finished that part. I told you I would help you all I could."

"Have I been here three days, then?" asked Colin, in astonishment.

"And nights too. And I and Jenny and the spindle are quite tired and want to sleep. Jenny has got three eggs to lay besides. Make haste, my boy."

"Please, then, tell me what I am to do next."

"Jenny will put you in the way. When you come where you are going, you will tell them that the old woman with the spindle desires them to lift Cumberbone Crag a yard higher, and to send a flue under Stonestarvit Moss. Jenny, show Colin the way."

Jenny came out with a surly *cluck* and led him a good way across the heath by a path only a hen could have found. But she turned suddenly and walked home again.

IV: THE GOBLIN BLACKSMITH

COLIN could just perceive something suggestive of a track, which he followed till the sun went down. Then he saw a dim light before him, keeping his eye upon which, he came at last to a smithy, where, looking in at the open door, he saw a huge, humpbacked smith working a forehammer in each hand.

He grinned out of the middle of his breast when he saw Colin, and said, "Come in; come in: my youngsters will be glad of you."

He was an awful looking creature, with a great hare lip, and a red ball for a nose. Whatever he did—speak, or laugh, or sneeze—he did not stop working one moment. As often as the sparks flew in his face, he snapped at them with his eyes (which were the colour of a half-dead coal), now with this one, now with that; and the more sparks they got into them the brighter his eyes grew. The moment Colin entered, he took a huge bar of iron from the furnace, and began laying on it so with his two forehammers that he disappeared in a cloud of of sparks, and Colin had to shut his eyes and be glad to escape with a few burns on his face and hands. When he had beaten the iron till it was nearly black, the smith put it in the fire again, and called out a hundred odd names:

"Here Gob, Shag, Latchit, Licker, Freestone, Greywhackit, Mousetrap, Potatoe-pot, Blob, Blotch, Blunker——"

And ever as he called, one dwarf after another came tumbling out of the chimney in the corner of which the fire was roaring. They crowded about Colin and began to make hideous faces and spit fire at him. But he kept a bold countenance. At length one pinched him, and he could not stand that, but struck him hard on the head. He thought he had knocked his own hand to pieces, it gave him such a jar; and the head rung like an iron pot.

"Come, come, young man," cried the smith; "you keep your hands off my children."

"Tell them to keep their hands off me, then," said Colin.

And calling to mind his message, just as they began to crowd about him again with yet more spiteful looks, he added—

"Here, you imps! I won't stand it longer. Get to your work directly. The old woman with the spindle says you're to lift Cumberbone Crag a yard higher, and to send a flue under Stonestarvit Moss."

In a moment they had vanished in the chimney. In a moment more the smithy rocked to its foundations. But the smith took no notice, only worked more furiously than ever. Then came a great crack and a shock that threw Colin on the floor. The smith reeled, but never lost hold of his hammers or missed a blow on the anvil.

"Those boys will do themselves a mischief," he said; then turning to Colin, "Here, you sir, take that hammer. This is no safe place for idle people. If you don't work you'll be knocked to pieces in no time."

The same moment there came a wind from the chimney that blew all the fire into the middle of the smithy. The smith dashed up upon the forge, and rushed out of sight. Presently he returned with one of the goblins under his arm kicking and screaming, laid his ugly head down on the anvil, where he held him by the neck, and hit him a great blow with his hammer above the ear. The hammer rebounded, the goblin gave a shriek, and the smith flung him into the chimney, saying—

"That's the only way to serve *him*. You'll be more careful for one while, I guess, Slobberkin."

And thereupon he took up his other hammer and began to work again, saying to Colin,

"Now, young man, as long as you get a blow with your hammer in for every one of mine, you'll be quite safe; but if you stop, or lose the beat, I won't be answerable to the old woman with the spindle for the consequences."

Colin took up the hammer and did his best. But he soon found that he had never known what it was to work. The smith worked a hammer in each hand,

and it was all Colin could do to work his little hammer with both his hands; so it was a terrible exertion to put in blow for blow with the smith. Once, when he lost the time, the smith's forehammer came down on the head of his, beat it flat on the anvil, and flung the handle to the other end of the smithy, where it struck the wall like the report of a cannon.

"I told you," said the smith. "There's another. Make haste, for the boys will be in want of you and me too before they get Cumberbone Crag half a foot higher."

Presently in came the biggest-headed of the family, out of the chimney.

"Six-foot wedges, and a three-yard crowbar!" he said; "or Cumberbone will cumber our bones presently."

The smith rushed behind the bellows, brought out a bar of iron three inches thick or so, cut off three yards, put the end in the fire, blew with might and main, and brought it out as white as paper. He and Colin then laid upon it till the end was flattened to an edge, which the smith turned up a little. He then handed the tool to the imp.

"Here, Gob," he said; "run with it, and the wedges will be ready by the time you come back."

Then to the wedges they set. And Colin worked like three. He never knew how he could work before. Not a moment's pause, except when the smith was at the forge for another glowing mass! And yet, to Colin's amazement, the more he worked the stronger he seemed to grow. Instead of being worn out, the moment he had got his breath he wanted to be at it again; and he felt as if he had grown twice the size since he took hammer in hand. And the goblins kept running in and out all the time, now for one thing, now for another. Colin thought if they made use of all the tools they fetched, they must be working very hard indeed: And the convulsions felt in the smithy bore witness to their exertions somewhere in the neighbourhood.

And the longer they worked together, the more friendly grew the smith. At length he said—his words always adding energy to his blows—

"What does the old woman want to improve Stone-starvit Moss for?"

"I didn't know she did want to improve it," returned Colin.

"Why, anybody may see that. First, she wants Cumberbone Crag a yard higher—just enough to send the north-east blast over the Moss without touching it. Then she wants a hot flue passed under it. Plain as a fore-hammer!—What did you ask her to do for you? She's always doing things for people and making my bones ache."

"You don't seem to mind it much, though, sir," said Colin.

"No more I do," answered the smith, with a blow that drove the anvil half way into the earth, from which it took him some trouble to drag it out again. "But I want to know what she is after now."

So Colin told him all he knew about it, which was merely his own story.

"I see, I see," said the smith. It's all moonshine; but we must do as she says notwithstanding. And now it is my turn to give you a lift, for you have worked well.—As soon as you leave the smithy, go straight to Stonestarvit Moss. Get on the highest part of it; make a circle three yards across, and dig a trench round it. I will give you a spade. At the end of the first day you will see a vine break the earth. By the end of the second, it will be creeping all over the circle. And by the end of the third day, the grapes will be ripe. Squeeze them one by one into a bottle—I will give you a bottle—till it is full. Cork it up tight, and by the time the queen comes for it, it will be Carasoyn."

"Oh, thank you, thank you," cried Colin. "When am I to go?"

"As soon as the boys have lifted Cumberbone Crag, and bored the flue under the Moss. It is of no use till then."

"Well, I'll go on with my work," said Colin, and struck away at the anvil.

In a minute or two in came the same goblin whose head his father had hammered, and said, respectfully,

"It's all right, sir. The boys are gathering their tools, and will be home to supper directly."

"Are you sure you have lifted the Crag a yard?" said the smith.

"Slumkin says it's a half-inch over the yard. Grungle says it's three-quarters. But that won't matter—will it?"

"No. I dare say not. But it is much better to be accurate. Is the flue done?"

"Yes, we managed that partly in lifting the crag."

"Very well. How's your head?"

"It rings a little."

"Let it ring you a lesson, then, Slobberkin, in future."

"Yes, sir."

"Now, master, you may go when you like," said the smith to Colin. "We've nothing here you can eat, I am sorry to say."

"Oh, I don't mind that. I'm not very hungry. But the old woman with the spindle said I was to work three days without dreaming."

"Well, you haven't been dreaming—have you?"

And the smith looked quite furious as he put the question, lifting his forehammer as if he would serve Colin like Slobberkin.

"No, that I haven't," answered Colin. "You took good care of that, sir."

The smith actually smiled.

"Then go along," he said. "It is all right."

"But I've only worked—"

"Three whole days and nights," interrupted the smith. "Get along with you. The boys will bother you if you don't. Here's your spade and here's your bottle."

V: THE MOSS VINEYARD

COLIN did not need a hint more, but was out of the smithy in a moment. He turned, however, to ask the way: there was nothing in sight but a great heap of peats which had been dug out of the moss, and was standing there to dry. Could he be on Stone-starvit Moss already? The sun was just setting. He would look out for the highest point at once. So he kept climbing, and at last reached a spot whence he could see all round him for a long way. Surely that must be Cumberbone Crag looking down on him! And there at his feet lay one of Jenny's eggs, as bright as silver. And there was a little path trodden and scratched by Jenny's feet, inclosing a circle just the size the smith told him to make. He set to work at once, ate Jenny's egg, and then dug the trench.

Those three days were the happiest he had ever known. For he understood everything he did himself, and all that everything was doing round about him. He saw what the rushes were, and why the blossom came out at the side, and why it was russet-coloured, and why the pitch was white, and the skin green. And he said to himself, "If I were a rush now, that's just how I should make a point of growing." And he knew how the heather felt with its cold roots, and its head of purple bells; and the wise-looking cotton-grass, which the old woman called her sheep, and the white beard of which she spun into thread. And he knew what she spun it for: namely, to weave it into lovely white cloth of which to make nightgowns for all the good people that were like to die; for one with one of these nightgowns upon him never died, but was laid in a beautiful white bed, and the door was closed upon him, and no noise came near him, and he lay there, dreaming lovely cool dreams, till the world had turned round, and was ready for him to get up again and do something.

He felt the wind playing with every blade of grass in his charmed circle. He felt the rays of heat shooting up from the hot flue beneath the moss. He knew the moment when the vine was going to break from the earth, and he felt the juices gathering and flowing from the roots into the grapes. And all the time he seemed at home, tending the cow, or making his father's supper, or reading a fairy tale as he sat waiting for him to come home.

At length the evening of the third day arrived. Colin squeezed the rich red grapes into his bottle, corked it, shouldered his spade, and turned homewards, guided by a peak which he knew in the distance. After walking all night in the moonlight, he came at length upon a place which he recognized, and so down upon the brook, which he followed home.

He met his father going out with his sheep. Great was his delight to see Colin again, for he had been dreadfully anxious about him. Colin told him the whole story; and as at that time marvels were much easier to believe than they are now, Colin's father did not laugh at him, but went away to the hills thinking, while Colin went on to the cottage, where he found plenty to do, having been nine days gone. He laid the bottle carefully away with his Sunday clothes, and set about everything just as usual.

But though the fairy brook was running merrily as

ever through the cottage, and although Colin watched late every night, and latest when the moon shone, no fairy fleet came glimmering and dancing in along the stream. Autumn was there at length, and cold fogs began to rise in the cottage, and so Colin turned the brook into its old course, and filled up the breaches in the walls and the channel along the floor, making all close against the blasts of winter. But he had never known such a weary winter before. He could not help constantly thinking how cold the little girl must be, and how she would be saying to herself, "I wish Colin hadn't been so silly and lost me."

VI: THE CONSEQUENCES

BUT at last the spring came, and after the spring the summer. And the very first warm day, Colin took his spade and pickaxe, and down rushed the stream once more, singing and bounding into the cottage. Colin was even more delighted than he had been the first time. And he watched late into the night, but there came neither moon nor fairy fleet. And more than a week passed thus.

At length, on the ninth night, Colin, who had just fallen asleep, opened his eyes with sudden wakefulness, and behold! the room was all in a glimmer with moonshine and fairy glitter. The boats were rocking on the water, and the queen and her court had landed, and were dancing merrily on the earthen floor. He lost no time.

"Queen! queen!" he said, "I've got your bottle of Carasoyn."

The dance ceased in a moment, and the queen bounded upon the edge of his bed.

"I can't bear the look of your great, glaring, ugly eyes," she said. "I must make you less before I can talk to you."

So once more she laid her rush wand across his eyes, whereupon Colin saw them all six times the size they were before, and the queen went on:

"Where is the Carasoyn? Give it me."

"It is in my box under the bed. If your majesty will stand out of the way, I will get it for you."

The queen jumped on the floor, and Colin, leaning from the bed, pulled out his little box, and got out the bottle.

"There it is, your majesty," he said, but not offering it to her.

"Give it me directly," said the queen, holding out her hand.

"First give me my little girl," returned Colin, boldly.

"Do you dare to bargain with me?" said the queen, angrily.

"Your majesty deigned to bargain with me first," said Colin.

"But since then you tried to break all our necks. You made a wicked cataract out there on the other side of the garden. Our boats were all dashed to pieces, and we had to wait till our horses were fetched. If I had been killed, you couldn't have held me to my bargain, and I won't hold to it now."

"If you chose to go down my cataract—" began Colin.

"*Your* cataract!" cried the queen. "All the waters that run from Loch Lonely are mine, I can tell you—all the way to the sea."

"Except where they run through farmyards, your majesty."

"I'll rout you out of the country," said the queen.

"Meantime I'll put the bottle in the chest again," returned Colin.

The queen bit her lips with vexation.

"Come here, Changeling," she cried at length, in a flattering tone.

And the little girl came slowly up to her, and stood staring at Colin, with the tears in her eyes.

"Give me your hand, little girl," said he, holding out his.

She did so. It was cold as ice.

"Let go her hand," said the queen.

"I won't, said Colin. "She's mine."

"Give me the bottle then," said the queen.

"Don't," said the child.

But it was too late. The queen had it.

"Keep your girl," she cried, with an ugly laugh.

"Yes, keep me," cried the child.

The cry ended in a hiss.

Colin felt something slimy wriggling in his grasp, and looking down, saw that instead of a little girl he was holding a great writhing worm. He had almost flung it from him, but recovering himself, he grasped it tighter.

"If it's a snake, I'll choke it," he said. "If it's a girl, I'll keep her."

The same instant it changed to a little white rabbit, which looked him piteously in the face, and pulled to get its little forefoot out of his hand. But, though he tried not to hurt it, Colin would not let it go. Then the rabbit changed to a great black cat, with eyes that flashed green fire. She sputtered and spit and swelled her tail, but all to no purpose. Colin held fast. Then it was a wood pigeon, struggling and fluttering in terror to get its wing out of his hold. But Colin still held fast.

All this time the queen had been getting the cork out. The moment it yielded she gave a scream and dropped the bottle. The Carasoyn ran out, and a strange odour filled the cottage. The queen stood shivering and sobbing beside the bottle, and all her court came about her and shivered and sobbed too, and their faces grew ancient and wrinkled. Then the queen, bending and tottering like an old woman, led the way to the boats, and her courtiers followed her, limping and creeping and distorted. Colin stared in amazement. He saw them all go aboard, and he heard the sound of them like a far-off company of men and women crying bitterly. And away they floated down the stream, the rowers dipping no oar, but bending weeping over them, and letting the boats drift along the stream. They vanished from his sight, and the rush of the cataract came up on the night-wind louder than he had ever heard it before. —But alas! when he came to himself, he found his hand relaxed, and the dove flown. Once more there was nothing left but to cry himself asleep, as he well might.

In the morning he rose very wretched. But the moment he entered the cowhouse, there, beside the cow, on the milking stool, sat a lovely little girl, with just one white garment on her, crying bitterly.

"I am so cold," she said, sobbing.

He caught her up, ran with her into the house, put her into the bed, and ran back to the cow for a bowl of warm milk. This she drank eagerly, laid her head down, and fell fast asleep. Then Colin saw that though she must be eight years old by her own account, her face was scarcely older than that of a baby of as many months.

When his father came home you may be sure he stared to see the child in the bed. Colin told him what had happened. But his father said he had met a troop of gipsies on the hill that morning.

"And you were always a dreamer, Colin, even before you could speak."

"But don't you smell the Carasoyn still?" said Colin.

"I do smell something very pleasant, to be sure," returned his father; "but I think it is the wallflower on the top of the garden-wall. What a blossom there

104

is of it this year! I am sure there is nothing sweeter in all Fairyland, Colin."

Colin allowed that.

The little girl slept for three whole days. And for three days more she never said another word than "I am so cold!" But after that she began to revive a little, and to take notice of things about her. For three weeks she would taste nothing but milk from the cow, and would not move from the chimney-corner. By degrees, however, she began to help Colin a little with his house-work, and as she did so, her face gathered more and more expression; and she made such progress, that by the end of three months she could do everything as well as Colin himself, and certainly more neatly. Whereupon he gave up his duties to her, and went out with his father to learn the calling of a shepherd.

Thus things went on for three years. And Fairy, as they called her, grew lovelier every day, and looked up to Colin more and more every day.

At the end of the three years, his father sent him to an old friend of his, a schoolmaster. Before he left, he made Fairy promise never to go near the brook after sundown. He had turned it into its old channel the very day she came to them. And he begged his father especially to look after her when the moon was high, for then she grew very restless and strange, and her eyes looked as if she saw things other people could not see.

When the end of the other three years had come, the schoolmaster would not let Colin go home, but insisted on sending him to college. And there he remained for three years more.

When he returned at the end of that time, he found Fairy so beautiful and so wise, that he fell dreadfully in love with her. And Fairy found out that she had been in love with him since ever so long—she did not know how long. And Colin's father agreed that they should be married as soon as Colin should have a house to take her to. So Colin went away to London, and worked very hard, till at last he managed to get a little cottage in Devonshire to live in. Then he went back to Scotland and married Fairy. And he was very glad to get her away from the neighbourhood of a queen who was not to be depended upon.

VII: THE BANISHED FAIRIES

THOSE fairies had for a long time been doing wicked things. They had played many ill-natured pranks upon the human mortals; had stolen children upon whom they had no claim; had refused to deliver them up when they were demanded of them; had even terrified infants in their cradles; and, final proof of moral declension in fairies, had attempted to get rid of the obligations of their word, by all kinds of trickery and false logic.

It was not till they had sunk thus low that their queen began to long for the Carasoyn. She, no more than if she had been a daughter of Adam, could be happy while going on in that way; and, therefore, having heard of its marvellous virtues, and thinking it would stop her growing misery, she tried hard to procure it. For a hundred years she had tried in vain. Not till Colin arose did she succeed. But the Carasoyn was only for really good people, and therefore when the iron bottle which contained it was uncorked, she, and all her attendants, were, by the vapours thereof, suddenly changed into old men and women fairies. They crowded away weeping and lamenting, and Colin had as yet seen them no more.

For when the wickedness of any fairy tribe reaches its climax, the punishment that falls upon them is, that they are compelled to leave that part of the country where they and their ancestors have lived for more years than they can count, and wander away, driven by an inward restlessness, ever longing after the country they have left, but never able to turn round and go back to it, always thinking they will do so to-morrow, but when to-morrow comes, saying *to-mor-row* again, till at last they find, not their old home, but the place of their doom—that is, a place where their restlessness leaves them, and they find they can remain. This partial repose, however, springs from no satisfaction with the place; it is only that their inward doom ceases to drive them further. They sit down to weep, and to long after the country they have left.

This is not because the country to which they have been driven is ugly and inclement—it may or may not be such: it is simply because it is not *their* country. If it would be, and it must be, torture to the fairy of a harebell to go and live in a hyacinth—a torture quite analogous to which many human beings undergo from their birth to their death, and some of them longer, for anything I can tell—think what it must be for a tribe of fairies to have to go and live in a country quite different from that in and for which they were born. To the whole tribe the country is what the flower is to the individual; and when a fairy is born to whom the whole country is what the individual flower is to the individual fairy, then the fairy is king or queen of the fairies, and always makes a new nursery rhyme for the young fairies, which is never forgotten. When, therefore, a tribe is banished, it is long before they can settle themselves into their new quarters. Their clothes do not fit them, as it were. They are constantly wriggling themselves into harmony with their new circumstances—which is only another word for clothes—and never quite succeeding. It is their punishment—and something more. Consequently their temper is not always of the evenest; indeed, and in a word, they are as like human mortals as may well be, considering the differences between them.

In the present case, you would say it was surely no great hardship to be banished from the heathy hills, the bare rocks, the wee trotting burnies of Scotland, to the rich valleys, the wooded shores, the great rivers, the grand ocean of the south of Devon. You may say they could not have been very wicked when this was all their punishment. If you do, you must have studied the human mortals to no great purpose. You do not believe that a man may be punished by being made very rich? I do. Anyhow, these fairies were not of your opinion, *for they were in it.* In the splendour of their Devon banishment, they sighed for their bare Scotland. Under the leafy foliage of the Devonshire valleys, with the purple and green ocean before them, that had seen ships of a thousand builds, or on the shore rich with shells and many-coloured creatures, they longed for the clear, cold, pensive, open sides of the far-stretching heathy sweeps, to which a gray, wild, torn sea, with memories only of Norsemen, whales, and mermaids, cried aloud. For the big rivers, on which reposed great old hulks scarred with battle, they longed after the rocks and stones and rowan and birch-trees of the solitary burns. The country they had left might be an ill-favoured thing, but it was their own.

Now that which happens to the aspect of a country when the fairies leave it, is that a kind of deadness falls over the landscape. The traveller feels the wind as before, but it does not seem to refresh him. The child sighs over his daisy chain, and cannot find a red-tipped one amongst all that he has gathered. The cowslips have not half the honey in them. The wasps outnumber the bees. The horses come from the plough more tired at night, hanging their heads to their very hoofs as they plod homewards. The youth and the maiden, though perfectly happy when they meet, find the road to and from the trysting-place unaccountably long and dreary. The hawthorn-blossom is neither so white nor so red as it used to be, and the dark rough bark looks through and makes it ragged. The day is neither so warm nor the night so friendly as before. In a word, that something which no one can describe or be content to go without is missing. Everything is common-place. Everything falls short of one's expectations.

But it does not follow that the country to which the fairies are banished is so much richer and more beautiful for their presence. If that country has its own fairies, it needs no more, and Devon in especial has been rich in fairies from the time of the Phoenicians, and ever so long before that. But supposing there were no aborigines left to quarrel with, it takes centuries before the new immigration can fit itself into its new home. Until this comes about, the queerest things are constantly happening. For however could a convolvulus grow right with the soul of a Canterbury-bell inside it, for instance? The banished fairies are forced to do the best they can, and take the flowers the nearest they can find.

VIII: THEIR REVENGE

WHEN Colin and his wife settled then in their farm-house, the same tribe of fairies was already in the neighbourhood, and was not long in discovering who had come after them. An assembly was immediately called. Something must be done; but what, was disputed. Most of them thought only of revenge—to be taken upon the children. But the queen hesitated. Perhaps her sufferings had done her good. She suggested that before coming to any conclusion they should wait and watch the household.

In consequence of this resolution they began to frequent the house constantly, and sometimes in great numbers. But for a long time they could do the children no mischief. Whatever they tried turned out to their amusement. They were three, two girls and a boy; the girls nine and eight, and the boy three years old.

When they succeeded in enticing them beyond the home-boundaries, they would at one time be seized with an unaccountable panic, and turn and scurry home without knowing why; at another, a great butterfly or dragon fly, or some other winged and lovely creature, would dart past them, and away towards the house, and they after it, scampering; or the voice of their mother would be heard calling from the door. But at last their opportunity arrived.

One day the children were having such a game! The sisters had blindfolded their little brother, and were carrying him now on their backs, now in their arms, all about the place; now up stairs, talking about the rugged mountain paths they were climbing; now down again, filling him with the fancy that they were descending into a narrow valley; then they would set the tap of a rain-water barrel running, and represent that they were travelling along the bank of a rivulet. Now they were threading the depths of a great forest: and when the low of a cow reached them from a nigh field, that was the roaring of a lion or a tiger. At length they reached a lake into which the rivulet ran, and then it was necessary to take off his shoes and socks, that he might skim over the water on his bare feet, which they dipped and dabbled now in this tub, now in that, standing for farm and household purposes by the water-butt. The sisters kept their own imaginations alive by carrying him through all the strange places inside and outside of the house. When they told him they were ascending a precipice, they were, in fact, climbing a rather difficult ladder up to the door of the hayloft; when they told him they were traversing a pathless desert, they were, in fact, in a vast, empty place, a wide floor, used sometimes as a granary, with the rafters of the roof coming down to it on both sides, a place abundantly potent in their feelings to the generation of the desert in his; when they were wandering through a trackless forest, they were, in fact, winding about amongst the trees of a large orchard, which, in the moonlight, was vast enough for the fancy of any child. Had they uncovered his eyes at any moment, he would only have been seized with a wonder and awe of another sort, more overwhelming because more real, and more strange because not even in part bodied forth from his own brain.

In the course of the story, and while they bore the bare-footed child through the orchard, telling him they saw the fairies gliding about everywhere through the trees, not thinking that he believed every word they told him, they set him down, and the child suddenly opened his eyes. His sisters were gone. The moon was staring at him out of the sky, through the mossy branches of the apple-trees, which he thought looked like old women all about him, they were so thin and bony.

When the sisters, who had only for a moment run behind some of the trees, that they might cause him additional amazement, returned, he was gone. There was terrible lamentation in the house; but his father and mother, who were experienced in such matters, knew that the fairies must be in it, and cherished a hope that their son would yet be restored to them, though all their endeavours to find him were unavailing.

IX: THE FAIRY FIDDLER

THE father thought over many plans, but never came upon the right one. He did not know that they were the same tribe which had before carried away his wife when she was an infant. If he had, they might have done something sooner.

At length, one night, towards the close of seven years, about twelve o'clock, Colin suddenly opened his eyes, for he had been fast asleep and dreaming, and saw a few grotesque figures which he thought he must have seen before, dancing on the floor between him and the nearly extinguished fire. One of them had a violin, but when Colin first saw him he was not playing. Another of them was singing, and thus keeping the dance in time. This was what he sang, evidently addressed to the fiddler, who stood in the centre of the dance:—

> *"Peterkin, Peterkin, tall and thin,*
> *What have you done with his cheek and his chin?*
> *What have you done with his ear and his eye?*
> *Hearken, hearken, and hear him cry."*

Here Peterkin put his fiddle to his neck, and drew from it a wail just like the cry of a child, at which the dancers danced more furiously. Then he went on playing the tune the other had just sung, in accompaniment to his own reply:—

> *"Silversnout, Silversnout, short and stout,*
> *I have cut them off and plucked them out,*
> *And salted them down in the Kelpie's Pool,*
> *Because papa Colin is such a fool."*

Then the fiddle cried like a child again, and they danced more wildly than ever.

Colin, filled with horror, although he did not more than half believe what they were saying, sat up in bed and stared at them with fierce eyes, waiting to hear what they would say next. Silversnout now resumed his part:—

"Ho, ho! Ho! ho! and if he don't know,
And fish them out of the pool, so —so," —

here they all pretended to be hauling in a net as they danced.

"Before the end of the seven long years,
Sweet babe will be left without eyes or ears."

Then Peterkin replied:—

"Sweet babe will be left without cheek or chin,
Only a hole to put porridge in;
Porridge and milk, and haggis, and cakes:
Sweet babe will gobble till his stomach aches."

From this last verse, Colin knew that they must be Scotch fairies, and all at once recollected their figures as belonging to the multitude he had once seen frolicking in his father's cottage. It was now Silversnout's turn. He began:

"But never more shall Colin see
Sweet babe again upon his knee,
With or without his cheek or chin,
Except — —"

Here Silversnout caught sight of Colin's face staring at him from the bed, and with a shriek of laughter they all vanished, the tones of Peterkin's fiddle trailing after them through the darkness like the train of a shooting star.

X: THE OLD WOMAN AND HER HEN

NOW Colin had got the better of these fairies once, not by his own skill, but by the help of that other powers had afforded him. What were those powers? First the old woman on the heath. Indeed, he might attribute it all to her. He would go back to Scotland and look for her and find her. But the old woman was never found except by the seeker losing himself. It could not be done otherwise. She would cease to be the old woman, and become her own hen, if ever the moment arrived when any one found her without losing himself. And Colin since that time had wandered so much all over the moor, wide as it was, that lay above his father's cottage, that he did not believe he was able to lose himself there any more. He had yet to learn that it did not so much matter where he lost himself, provided only he was lost.

Just at this time Colin's purse was nearly empty, and he set out to borrow the money of a friend who lived on the other side of Dartmoor. When he got there, he found that he had gone from home. Unable to rest, he set out again to return.

It was almost night when he started, and before he had got many miles into the moor, it was dark, for there was no moon, and it was so cloudy that he could not see the stars. He thought he knew the way quite well, but as the track even in daylight was in certain places very indistinct, it was no wonder that he strayed from it, and found that he had lost himself. The same moment that he became aware of this, he saw a light away to the left. He turned towards it and found it proceeded from a little hive-like hut, the door of which stood open. When he was within a yard or two of it, he heard a voice say—

"Come in, Colin; I'm waiting for you."

Colin obeyed at once, and found the old woman

seated with her spindle and distaff, just as he had seen her when he was a boy on the moor above his father's cottage.

"How do you do, mother?" he said.

"I am always quite well. Never ask me that question."

"Well, then I won't any more," returned Colin. "But I thought you lived in Scotland?"

"I don't live anywhere; but those that will do as I tell them, will always find me when they want me."

"Do you see yet, mother?"

"See! I always see so well that it is not worth while to burn eyelight. So I let them go out. They were expensive."

Where her eyes should have been, there was nothing but wrinkles.

"What do you want?" she resumed.

"I want my child. The fairies have got him."

"I know that."

"And they have taken out his eyes."

"I can make him see without them."

"And they've cut off his ears," said Colin.

"He can hear without them."

"And they've salted down his cheek and his chin."

"Now I don't believe that," said the old woman.

"I heard them say so myself," returned Colin.

"Those fairies are worse liars than any I know. But something must be done. Sit down and I'll tell you a story."

"There's only nine days of the seven years left," said Colin, in a tone of expostulation.

"I know that as well as you," answered the old woman. "Therefore, I say, there is not time to be lost. Sit down and listen to my story. Here, Jenny."

The hen came pacing solemnly out from under the bed.

"Off to the sheep-shearing, Jenny, and make haste, for I must spin faster than usual. There are but nine days left."

Jenny ran out at the door with her head on a level with her tail, as if the kite had been after her. In a few moments she returned with a bunch of wool, as they called it, though it was only cotton from the cotton-grass that grew all about the cottage, nearly as big as herself, in her bill, and then darted away for more. The old woman fastened it on her distaff, drew out a thread to her spindle, and then began to spin. And as she spun she told her story—fast, fast; and Jenny kept scampering out and in; and by the time Colin thought it must be midnight, the story was told, and seven of the nine days were over.

"Colin," said the old woman, "now that you know all about it, you must set off at once."

"I am ready," answered Colin, rising.

"Keep on the road Jenny will show you till you come to the cobbler's. Tell him the old woman with the distaff requests him to give you a lump of his wax."

"And what am I to do with it?"

"The cobbler always knows what his wax is for."

And with this answer, the old woman turned her face towards the fire, for, although it was summer, it was cold at night on the moor. Colin, moved by sudden curiosity, instead of walking out of the hut after Jenny, as he ought to have done, crept round by the wall, and peeped in the old woman's face. There, instead of wrinkled blindness, he saw a pair of flashing orbs of light, which were rather reflected on the fire than had the fire reflected in them. But the same instant the hut and all that was in it vanished, he felt the cold fog of the moor blowing upon him, and fell heavily to the earth.

XI: THE GOBLIN COBBLER

WHEN he came to himself he lay on the moor still. He got up and gazed around. The moon was up, but there was no hut to be seen. He was sorry enough now that he had been so foolish. He called, "Jenny, Jenny," but in vain. What was he to do? To-morrow was the eighth of the nine days left, and if before twelve at night the following day he had not rescued his boy, nothing could be done, at least for seven years more. True, the year was not quite out till about seven the following evening, but the fairies, instead of giving days of grace, always take them. He could do nothing but begin to walk, simply because that gave him a shadow more of a chance of finding the cobbler's than if he sat still, but there was no possibility of choosing one direction rather than another.

He wandered the rest of that night and the next day. He could not go home before the hour when the cobbler could no longer help him. Such was his anxiety, that although he neither ate nor drank, he never thought of the cause of his gathering weakness.

As it grew dark, however, he became painfully aware of it, and was just on the point of sitting down exhausted upon a great white stone that looked inviting, when he saw a faint glimmering in front of him. He was erect in a moment, and making towards the place. As he drew near he became aware of a noise made up of many smaller noises, such as might have proceeded from some kind of factory. Not till he was close to the place could he see that it was a long low hut, with one door, and no windows. The light shone from the door, which stood wide open. He approached, and peeped in. There sat a multitude of cobblers, each on his stool, with his candle stuck in the hole in the seat, cobbling away. They looked rather

117

little men, though not at all of fairy-size. The most remarkable thing about them was, that at any given moment they were all doing precisely the same thing, as if they had been a piece of machinery. When one drew the threads in stitching, they all did the same. If Colin saw one wax his thread, and looked up, he saw that they were all waxing their thread. If one took to hammering on his lapstone, they did not follow his example, but all together with him they caught up their lapstones and fell to hammering away, as if nothing but hammering could ever be demanded of them. And when he came to look at them more closely, he saw that every one was blind of an eye, and had a nose turned up like an awl. Every one of them, however, looked different from the rest, notwithstanding a very close resemblance in their features.

The moment they caught sight of him, they rose as one man, pointed their awls at him, and advanced towards him like a closing bush of aloes, glittering with spikes.

"Fine upper-leathers," said one and all, with a variety of accordant grimaces.

"Top of his head—good paste-bowl," was the next general remark.

"Coarse hair—good ends," followed.

"Sinews—good thread."

"Bones and blood—good paste for seven-leaguers."

"Ears—good loops to pull 'em on with. Pair short now."

"Soles—same for queen's slippers."

And so on they went, portioning out his body in the most irreverent fashion for the uses of their trade, till having come to his teeth, and said—

"Teeth—good brads,"—they all gave a shriek like the whisk of the waxed threads through the leather, and sprung upon him with their awls drawn back like daggers. There was no time to lose.

"The old woman with the spindle——" said Colin.

"Don't know her," shrieked the cobblers.

"The old woman with the distaff," said Colin, and they all scurried back to their seats and fell to hammering vigorously.

"She desired me," continued Colin, "to ask the cobbler for a lump of his wax."

Every one of them caught up his lump of wrought rosin, and held it out to Colin. He took the one offered by the nearest, and found that all their lumps were gone; after which they sat motionless and stared at him.

"But what am I to do with it?" asked Colin.

"I will walk a little way with you," said the one nearest, "and tell you all about it. The old woman is my grandmother, and a very worthy old soul she is."

Colin stepped out at the door of the workshop, and the cobbler followed him. Looking round, Colin saw all the stools vacant, and the place as still as an old churchyard. The cobbler, who now in his talk, gestures, and general demeanour appeared a very respectable, not to say conventional, little man, proceeded to give him all the information he required, accompanying it with the present of one of his favourite awls.

They walked a long way, till Colin was amazed to find that his strength stood out so well. But at length the cobbler said—

"I see, sir, that the sun is at hand. I must return to my vocation. When the sun is once up, you will know where you are."

He turned aside a few yards from the path, and entered the open door of a cottage. In a moment the place resounded with the soft hammering of three hundred and thirteen cobblers, each with his candle stuck in a hole in the stool on which he sat. While Colin stood gazing in wonderment, the rim of the sun

119

crept up above the horizon; and there the cottage
stood, white and sleeping, while the cobblers, their
lights, their stools, and their tools had all vanished.
Only there was still the sound of the hammers ringing
in his head, where it seemed to shape itself into words
something like these: a good deal had to give way to
the rhyme, for they were more particular about their
rhymes than their etymology:

> "Dub-a-dub, dub-a-dub,
> Cobbler's man
> Hammer it, stitch it,
> As fast as you can.
> The week-day ogre
> Is wanting his boots;
> The trip-a-trap fairy
> Is going bare-foots.
> Dream-daughter has worn out
> Her heels and her toeses,
> For want of cork slippers
> To walk over noses.
> Spark-eye, the smith,
> May shoe the nightmare,
> The kelpie and pookie,
> The nine-footed bear:
> We shoe the mermaids —
> The tips of their tails —
> Stitching the leather
> Onto their scales.
> We shoe the brownie,
> Clumsy and toeless,
> And then he goes quiet
> As a mole or a moless.

There is but one creature
That we cannot shoe,
And that is the Boneless,
All made of glue."

A great deal of nonsense of this sort went through Colin's head before the sounds died away. Then he found himself standing in the field outside his own orchard.

XII: THE WAX AND THE AWL

THE evening arrived. The sun was going down over the sea, cloudless, casting gold from him lavishly, when Colin arrived on the shore at some distance from his home. The tide was falling, and a good space of sand was uncovered, and lay glittering in the setting sun. This sand lay between some rocks and the sea; and from the rocks innumerable runnels of water that had been left behind in their hollows were hurrying back to their mother. These occasionally spread into little shallow lakes, resting in hollows in the sand. These lakes were in a constant ripple from the flow of the little streams through them; and the sun shining on these multitudinous ripples, the sand at the bottom shone like brown silk watered with gold, only that the golden lines were flitting about like living things, never for a moment in one place.

Now Colin had no need of fairy ointment to anoint his eyes and make him able to see fairies. Most people need this; but Colin was naturally gifted. Therefore, as he drew near a certain high rock, which he knew very well, and from which many streams were flowing back into the sea, he saw that the little lakes about it were crowded with fairies, playing all kinds of pranks in the water. It was a lovely sight to see them thus frolicking in the light of the setting sun,

121

in their gay dresses, sparkling with jewels, or what looked like jewels, flashing all colours as they moved. But Colin had not much time to see them; for the moment they saw him, knowing that this was the man whom they had wronged by stealing his child, and knowing too that he saw them, they fled at once up the high rock and vanished. This was just what Colin wanted. He went all round and round the rock, looked in every direction in which there might be a pool, found more fairies, here and there, who fled like the first up the rock and disappeared. When he had thus driven them all from the sands, he approached the rock, taking the lump of cobbler's wax from his pocket as he went. He scrambled up the rock, and, without showing his face, put his hand on the uppermost edge of it, and began drawing a line with the wax all along. He went creeping round the rock, still drawing the wax along the edge, till he had completed the circuit. Then he peeped over.

Now in the heart of this rock, which was nearly covered at highwater, there was a big basin, known as the Kelpie's Pool, filled with sea-water and the loveliest sea-weed and many little sea-animals; and this was a favourite resort of the fairies. It was now, of course, crowded. When they saw his big head come peeping over, they burst into a loud fit of laughter, and began mocking him and making game of him in a hundred ways. Some made the ugliest faces they could, some queer gestures of contempt; others sung bits of songs, and so on; while the queen sat by herself on a projecting corner of the rock, with her feet in the water, and looked at him sulkily. Many of them kept on plunging and swimming and diving and floating, while they mocked him; and Colin would have enjoyed the sight much if they had not spoiled their beauty and their motions by their grimaces and their gestures.

"I want my child," said Colin.

"Give him his child," cried one.

Thereupon a dozen of them dived, and brought up a huge sea-slug—a horrid creature, like a lump of blubber—and held it up to him, saying—

"There he is; come down and fetch him."

Others offered him a blue lobster, struggling in their grasp; others, a spider-crab; others, a whelk; while some of them sung mocking verses, each capping the line the other gave. At length they lifted a dreadful object from the bottom. It was like a baby with his face half eaten away by the fishes, only that he had a huge nose, like the big toe of a lobster. But Colin was not to be taken in.

"Very well, good people," he said, "I will try something else."

He crept down the rock again, took out the little cobbler's awl, and began boring a hole. It went through the rock as if it had been butter, and as he drew it out the water followed in a far-reaching spout. He bored another, and went on boring till there were three hundred and thirteen spouts gushing from the rock, and running away in a strong little stream towards the sea. He then sat down on a ledge at the foot of the rock and waited.

By-and-by he heard a clamour of little voices from the basin. They had found that the water was getting very low. But when they discovered the holes by which it was escaping, "He's got Dottlecob's awl! He's got Dottlecob's awl!" they cried with one voice of horror. When he heard this, Colin climbed the rock again to enjoy their confusion. But here I must explain a little.

In the former part of this history I showed how fond these fairies were of water. But the fact was, they were far too fond of it. It had grown a thorough dissipation with them. Their business had been chiefly to tend and help the flowers in which they lived, and to do good offices for every thing that had any kind of life about them. Hence their name of Good People. But from finding the good the water did to the flowers, and from sharing in the refreshment it brought them, flowing up to them in tiny runnels through the veins of the plants, they had fallen in love with the water itself, for its own sake, or rather for the pleasure it gave to them, irrespective of the good it was to the flowers which lived upon it. So they neglected their business, and took to sailing on the streams, and plunging into every pool they could find. Hence the rapidity of their decline and fall.

Again, on coming to the sea-coast, they had found that the salt water did much to restore the beauty they had lost by partaking of the Carasoyn. Therefore they were constantly on the shore, bathing for ever in the water, especially that left in this pool by the ebbing tide, which was particularly to their taste; till at last they had grown entirely dependent for comfort on the sea-water, and, they thought, entirely dependent on it for existence also, at least such existence as was in the least worth possessing.

Therefore, when they saw the big face of Colin peering once more over the ledge, they rushed at him in a rage, scrambling up the side of the rock like so many mad beetles. Colin drew back and let them come on. The moment the foremost put his foot on the line that Colin had drawn around the rock, he slipped and tumbled backwards head over heels into the pool, shrieking—

"He's got Dottlecob's wax!"

"He's got Dottlecob's wax!" screamed the next, as he fell backwards after his companion, and this took place till no one would approach the line. In fact no fairy could keep his footing on the wax, and the line was so broad—for as Colin rubbed it, it had melted and spread—that not one of them could spring over it. The queen now rose.

"What do you want, Colin?" she said.

"I want my child, as you know very well," answered Colin.

"Come and take him," returned the queen, and sat down again, not now with her feet in the water, for it was much too low for that.

But Colin knew better. He sat down on the edge of the basin. Unfortunately, the tail of his coat crossed the line. In a moment half-a-dozen of the fairies were out of the circle. Colin rose instantly, and there was not much harm done, for the multitude was still in prison. The water was nearly gone, beginning to leave the very roots of the long tangles uncovered. At length the queen could bear it no longer.

"Look here, Colin," she said; "I wish you well."

And as she spoke she rose and descended the side of the rock towards the water now far below her. She had to be very cautious too, the stones were so slippery, though there was none of Dottlecob's wax there. About half-way below where the surface of the pool had been, she stopped, and pushed a stone aside. Colin saw what seemed the entrance to a cave inside the rock. The queen went in. A few moments after she came out wringing her hands.

"Oh dear! oh dear! What shall I do?" she cried, "You horrid thick people will grow so. He's grown to such a size that I *can't* get him out."

"Will you let him go if I get him out?" asked Colin.

"I will, I will. We shall all be starved to death for want of sea-water if I don't," she answered.

"Swear by the cobbler's awl and the cobbler's wax," said Colin.

"I swear," said the queen.

"By the cobbler's awl and the cobbler's wax," insisted Colin.

"I swear by the cobbler's awl and the cobbler's wax," returned the queen.

"In the name of your people?"

"In the name of my people," said the queen, "that none of us here present will ever annoy you or your family hereafter."

"Then I'll come down," said Colin, and jumped into the basin. With the cobbler's awl he soon cleared a big opening into the rock, for it bored and cut it like butter. Then out crept a beautiful boy of about ten years old, into his father's arms, with eyes, and ears, and chin, and cheek all safe and sound. And he carried him home to his mother.

It was a disappointment to find him so much of a baby at his age; but that fault soon began to mend. And the house was full of jubilation. And little Colin told them the whole story of his sojourn among the fairies. And it did not take so long as you would think, for he fancied he had been there only about a week.

PORT IN A STORM

PAPA," said my sister Effie, one evening as we all sat about the drawing-room fire. One after another, as nothing followed, we turned our eyes upon her. There she sat, still silent, embroidering the corner of a cambric handkerchief, apparently unaware that she had spoken.

It was a very cold night in the beginning of winter. My father had come home early, and we had dined early that we might have a long evening together, for it was my father's and mother's wedding-day, and we always kept it as the homeliest of holidays. My father was seated in an easy-chair by the chimney corner, with a jug of Burgundy near him, and my mother sat by his side, now and then taking a sip out of his glass.

Effie was now nearly nineteen; the rest of us were younger. What she was thinking about we did not know then, though we could all guess now. Suddenly she looked up, and seeing all eyes fixed upon her, became either aware or suspicious, and blushed rosy red.

"You spoke to me, Effie. What was it, my dear?"

"O yes, papa. I wanted to ask you whether you wouldn't tell us, to-night, the story about how you——"

"Well, my love?"

"—About how you——"

Reprinted from *Argosy* (1866).

"I am listening, my dear."

"I mean, about mamma and you."

"Yes, yes. About how I got your mamma for a mother to you. Yes. I paid a dozen of port for her."

We all and each exlaimed *Papa!* and my mother laughed.

"Tell us all about it," was the general cry.

"Well, I will," answered my father. "I must begin at the beginning, though."

And, filling his glass with Burgundy, he began.

"As far back as I can remember, I lived with my father in an old manor-house in the country. It did not belong to my father, but to an elder brother of his, who at that time was captain of a seventy-four. He loved the sea more than his life; and, as yet apparently, had loved his ship better than any woman. At least he was not married.

"My mother had been dead for some years, and my father was now in very delicate health. He had never been strong, and since my mother's death, I believe, though I was too young to notice it, he had pined away. I am not going to tell you anything about him just now, because it does not belong to my story. When I was about five years old, as nearly as I can judge, the doctors advised him to leave England. The house was put into the hands of an agent to let—at least, so I suppose; and he took me with him to Madeira, where he died. I was brought home by his servant, and by my uncle's directions, sent to a boarding-school; from there to Eton, and from there to Oxford.

"Before I had finished my studies, my uncle had been an admiral for some time. The year before I left Oxford, he married Lady Georgiana Thornbury, a widow lady, with one daughter. Thereupon he bade farewell to the sea, though I dare say he did not like the parting, and retired with his bride to the house where he was born—the same house I told you I was born in, which had been in the family for many generations, and which your cousin now lives in.

"It was late in the autumn when they arrived at Culverwood. They were no sooner settled than my uncle wrote to me, inviting me to spend Christmas-tide with them at the old place. And here you may see my story has arrived at its beginning.

"It was with strange feelings that I entered the house. It looked so old-fashioned, and stately, and grand, to eyes which had been accustomed to all the modern commonplaces! Yet the shadowy recollections which hung about it gave an air of homeliness to the place, which, along with the grandeur, occasioned a sense of rare delight. For what can be better than to feel that you are in stately company, and at the same time perfectly at home in it? I am grateful to this day for the lesson I had from the sense of which I have spoken—that of mingled awe and tenderness in the aspect of the old hall as I entered it for the first time after fifteen years, having left it a mere child.

"I was cordially received by my old uncle and my new aunt. But the moment Kate Thornbury entered I lost my heart, and have never found it again to this day. I get on wonderfully well without it, though, for I have got the loan of a far better one till I find my own, which therefore, I hope I never shall."

My father glanced at my mother as he said this, and she returned his look in a way which I can now interpret as a quiet satisfied confidence. But the tears came in Effie's eyes. She had trouble before long, poor girl! But it is not her story I have to tell.—My father went on:

"Your mother was prettier then than she is now, but not so beautiful; beautiful enough, though, to make me think there never had been or could again

129

be anything so beautiful. She met me kindly, and I met her awkwardly."

"You made me feel that I had no business there," said my mother, speaking for the first time in the course of the story.

"See there, girls," said my father. "You are always so confident in first impressions, and instinctive judgment! I was awkward because, as I said, I fell in love with your mother the moment I saw her; and she thought I regarded her as an intruder into the old family precincts.

"I will not follow the story of the days. I was very happy, except when I felt too keenly how unworthy I was of Kate Thornbury; not that she meant to make me feel it, for she was never other than kind; but she was such that I could not help feeling it. I gathered courage, however, and before three days were over, I began to tell her all my slowly reviving memories of the place, with my childish adventures associated with this and that room or outhouse or spot in the grounds; for the longer I was in the place the more my old associations with it revived, till I was quite astonished to find how much of my history in connection with Culverwood had been thoroughly imprinted on my memory. She never showed, at least, that she was weary of my stories; which, however interesting to me, must have been tiresome to any one who did not sympathize with what I felt towards my old nest. From room to room we rambled, talking or silent; and nothing could have given me a better chance, I believe, with a heart like your mother's. I think it was not long before she began to like me, at least, and liking had every opportunity of growing into something stronger, if only she too did not come to the conclusion that I was unworthy of her.

"My uncle received me like the jolly old tar that he was—welcomed me to the old ship—hoped we should make many a voyage together—and that I would take the run of the craft—all but in one thing.

" 'You see, my boy,' he said, 'I married above my station, and I don't want my wife's friends to say that I laid alongside of her to get hold of her daughter's fortune. No, no, my boy; your old uncle has too much salt water in him to do a dog's trick like that. So you take care of yourself—that's all. She might turn the head of a wiser man than ever came out of our family.'

"I did not tell my uncle that his advice was already too late; for that, though it was not an hour since I had first seen her, my head was so far turned already, that the only way to get it right again, was to go on turning it in the same direction; though, no doubt, there was a danger of overhauling the screw. The old gentleman never referred to the matter again, nor took any notice of our increasing intimacy; so that I sometimes doubt even now if he could have been in earnest in the very simple warning he gave me. Fortunately, Lady Georgiana liked me—at least I thought she did, and that gave me courage."

"That's all nonsense, my dear," said my mother. "Mamma was nearly as fond of you as I was; but you never wanted courage."

"I knew better than to show my cowardice, I dare say," returned my father. "But," he continued, "things grew worse and worse, till I was certain I should kill myself, or go straight out of my mind, if your mother would not have me. So it went on for a few days, and Christmas was at hand.

"The admiral had invited several old friends to come and spend the Christmas week with him. Now you must remember that, although you look on me as an old-fashioned fogie——"

"Oh, papa!" we all interrupted; but he went on.

"Yet my old uncle was an older-fashioned fogie, and his friends were much the same as himself. Now,

I am fond of a glass of port, though I dare not take it, and must content myself with Burgundy. Uncle Bob would have called Burgundy pig-wash. *He* could not do without his port, though he was a moderate enough man, as customs were. Fancy, then, his dismay when, on questioning his butler, an old coxen of his own, and after going down to inspect in person, he found that there was scarcely more than a dozen of port in the wine-cellar. He turned white with dismay, and, till he had brought the blood back to his countenance by swearing, he was something awful to behold in the dim light of the tallow candle old Jacob held in his tattooed fist. I will not repeat the words he used; fortunately, they are out of fashion amongst gentlemen, although ladies, I understand, are beginning to revive the custom, now old, and always ugly. Jacob reminded his honour that he would not have more put down till he had got a proper cellar built, for the one there was, he had said, was not fit to put anything but dead men in. Thereupon, after abusing Jacob for not reminding him of the necessities of the coming season, he turned to me, and began, certainly not to swear at his own father, but to expostulate sideways with the absent shade for not having provided a decent cellar before his departure from this world of dinners and wine, hinting that it was somewhat selfish, and very inconsiderate of the welfare of those who were to come after him. Having a little exhausted his indignation, he came up, and wrote the most peremptory order to his wine-merchant, in Liverpool, to let him have thirty dozen of port before Christmas Day, even if he had to send it by post-chaise. I took the letter to the post myself, for the old man would trust nobody but me, and indeed would have preferred taking it himself; but in winter he was always lame from the effects of a bruise he had received from a falling spar in the battle of Aboukir.

"That night I remember well. I lay in bed wondering whether I might venture to say a word, or even to give a hint to your mother that there was a word that pined to be said if it might. All at once I heard a whine of the wind in the old chimney. How well I knew that whine! For my kind aunt had taken the trouble to find out what room I had occupied as a boy, and, by the third night I spent there, she had got it ready for me. I jumped out of bed, and found that the snow was falling fast and thick. I jumped into bed again, and began wondering what my uncle would do if the port did not arrive. And then I thought that, if the snow went on falling as it did, and if the wind rose any higher, it might turn out that the roads through the hilly part of Yorkshire in which Culverwood lay, might very well be blocked up.

"The north wind doth blow,
.   *And we shall have snow,*
And what will my uncle do then, poor thing?
He'll run for his port,
But he will run short,
And have too much water to drink, poor thing!

"With the influences of the chamber of my childhood crowding upon me, I kept repeating the travestied rhyme to myself, till I fell asleep.

"Now, boys and girls, if I were writing a novel, I should like to make you, somehow or other, put together the facts—that I was in the room I have mentioned; that I had been in the cellar with my uncle for the first time that evening; that I had seen my uncle's distress, and heard his reflections upon his father. I may add that I was not myself, even then, so indifferent to the merits of a good glass of port as to be unable to enter into my uncle's dismay, and that of his guests at last, if they should find that the snow-storm had actually closed up the sweet approaches of the expected port. If I was personally indifferent to the matter, I fear it is to be attributed to your mother, and not to myself."

"Nonsense!" interposed my mother once more. "I never knew such a man for making little of himself and much of other people. You never drank a glass too much port in your life."

"That's why I'm so fond of it, my dear," returned my father. "I declare you make me quite discontented with my pig-wash here.

"That night I had a dream.

"The next day the visitors began to arrive. Before the evening after, they had all come. There were five of them—three tars and two land-crabs, as they called each other when they got jolly, which, by-the-way, they would not have done long without me.

"My uncle's anxiety visibly increased. Each guest, as he came down to breakfast, received each morning a more constrained greeting.—I beg your pardon, la-dies; I forgot to mention that my aunt had lady-visi-tors, of course. But the fact is, it is only the port-drinking visitors in whom my story is interested, al-ways excepted your mother.

"These ladies my admiral uncle greeted with some-thing even approaching to servility. I understood him well enough. He instinctively sought to make a party to protect him when the awful secret of his cellar should be found out. But for two preliminary days or so, his resources would serve; for he had plenty of excellent claret and Madeira—stuff I don't know much about—and both Jacob and himself condescended to manoeuvre a little.

"The wine did not arrive. But the morning of Christmas Eve did. I was sitting in my room, trying to write a song for Kate—that's your mother, my dears——"

"I know, papa," said Effie, as if she were very knowing to know that.

"——when my uncle came into the room, looking like Sintram with Death and the Other One after him—that's the nonsense you read to me the other day, isn't it, Effie?"

"Not nonsense, dear papa," remonstrated Effie; and I loved her for saying it, for surely *that* is not nonsense.

"I didn't mean it," said my father; and turning to my mother, added: "It must be your fault, my dear, that my children are so serious that they always take a joke for earnest. However, it was no joke with my uncle. If he didn't look like Sintram he looked like t'other one.

" 'The roads are frozen—I mean snowed up,' he said. 'There's just one bottle of port left, and what Captain Calker will say—I dare say I know, but I'd rather not. Damn this weather!—God forgive me!—that's not right—but it *is* trying—ain't it, my boy?'

" 'What will you give me for a dozen of port, uncle?' was all my answer.

" 'Give you? I'll give you Culverwood, you rogue.'

" 'Done,' I cried.

" 'That is,' stammered my uncle, 'that is,' and he reddened like the funnel of one of his hated steamers, 'that is, you know, always provided, you know. It wouldn't be fair to Lady Georgiana, now, would it? I put it to yourself—if she took the trouble, you know. You understand me, my boy?'

" 'That's of course, uncle,' I said.

" 'Ah! I see you're a gentleman like your father, not to trip a man when he stumbles,' said my uncle. For such was the dear old man's sense of honour, that he was actually uncomfortable about the hasty promise he had made without first specifying the exception. The exception, you know, has Culverwood at the present hour, and right welcome he is.

" 'Of course, uncle,' I said—'between gentlemen, you know. Still, I want my joke out, too. What will you give me for a dozen of port to tide you over Christmas Day?'

" 'Give you, my boy? I'll give you——'

"But here he checked himself, as one that had been burned already.

" 'Bah!' he said, turning his back, and going towards the door; 'what's the use of joking about serious affairs like this?'

"And so he left the room. And I let him go. For I had heard that the road from Liverpool was impassable, the wind and snow having continued every day since that night of which I told you. Meantime, I had never been able to summon the courage to say one word to your mother—I beg her pardon, I mean Miss Thornbury.

"Christmas Day arrived. My uncle was awful to behold. His friends were evidently anxious about him. They thought he was ill. There was such a hesitation about him, like a shark with a bait, and such a flurry, like a whale in his last agonies. He had a horrible secret which he dared not tell, and which yet *would* come out of its grave at the appointed hour.

"Down in the kitchen the roast beef and turkey were meeting their deserts. Up in the store-room—for Lady Georgiana was not above housekeeping, any more than her daughter—the ladies of the house were doing their part; and I was oscillating between my uncle and his niece, making myself amazingly useful now to one and now to the other. The turkey and the beef were on the table, nay, they had been well eaten, before I felt that my moment was come. Outside, the wind was howling, and driving the snow with soft pats against the window-panes. Eager-eyed I watched

General Fortescue, who despised sherry or Madeira even during dinner, and would no more touch champagne than he would *eau sucrée,* but drank port after fish or with cheese indiscriminately—with eager eyes I watched how the last bottle dwindled out its fading life in the clear decanter. Glass after glass was supplied to General Fortescue by the fearless cockswain, who, if he might have had his choice, would rather have boarded a Frenchman than waited for what was to follow. My uncle scarcely ate at all, and the only thing that stopped his face from growing longer with the removal of every dish was that nothing but death could have made it longer than it was already. It was my interest to let matters go as far as they might up to a certain point, beyond which it was not my interest to let them go, if I could help it. At the same time I was curious to know how my uncle would announce—confess the terrible fact that in his house, on Christmas Day, having invited his oldest friends to share with him the festivities of the season, there was not one bottle more of port to be had.

"I waited till the last moment—till I fancied the admiral was opening his mouth, like a fish in despair, to make his confession. He had not even dared to make a confidante of his wife in such an awful dilemma. Then I pretended to have dropped my table-napkin behind my chair, and rising to seek it, stole round behind my uncle, and whispered in his ear:

" 'What will you give me for a dozen of port now, uncle?'

" 'Bah!' he said, 'I'm at the gratings; don't torture me.'

" 'I'm in earnest, uncle.'

"He looked round at me with a sudden flash of bewildered hope in his eye. In the last agony he was capable of believing in a miracle. But he made me no reply. He only stared.

" 'Will you give me Kate? I want Kate,' I whispered.

" 'I will, my boy. That is, if she'll have you. That is, I mean to say, if you produce the true tawny.'

" 'Of course, uncle; honour bright—as port in a storm,' I answered, trembling in my shoes and everything else I had on, for I was not more than three parts confident in the result.

"The gentlemen beside Kate happening at the moment to be occupied, each with the lady on his other side, I went behind her, and whispered to her as I had whispered to my uncle, though not exactly in the same terms. Perhaps I had got a little courage from the champagne I had drunk; perhaps the excitement of the whole venture kept me up; perhaps Kate herself gave me courage, like a goddess of old, in some way I did not understand. At all events I said to her:

" 'Kate,'—we had got so far even then—'my uncle hasn't another bottle of port in his cellar. Consider what a state General Fortescue will be in soon. He'll be tipsy for want of it. Will you come and help me to find a bottle or two?'

"She rose at once, with a white-rose blush—so delicate. I don't believe any one saw it but myself. But the shadow of a stray ringlet could not fall on her cheek without my seeing it.

"When we got into the hall, the wind was roaring loud, and the few lights were flickering and waving gustily with alternate light and shade across the old portraits which I had known so well as a child—for I used to think what each would say first, if he or she came down out of the frame and spoke to me.

"I stopped, and taking Kate's hand, I said—

" 'I daren't let you come farther, Kate, before I tell you another thing: my uncle has promised, if I find him a dozen of port—you must have seen what a state the poor man is in—to let me say something to you—I suppose he meant your mamma, but I prefer saying it to you, if you will let me. Will you come and help me to find the port?'

"She said nothing, but took up a candle that was on a table in the hall, and stood waiting. I ventured to look at her. Her face was now celestial rosy red, and I could not doubt that she had understood me. She looked so beautiful that I stood staring at her without moving. What the servants could have been about that not one of them crossed the hall, I can't think.

"At last Kate laughed and said—'Well?' I started, and I dare say took my turn at blushing. At least I did not know what to say. I had forgotten all about the guests inside. 'Where's the port?' said Kate. I caught hold of her hand again and kissed it."

"You needn't be quite so minute in your account, my dear," said my mother, smiling.

"I will be more careful in future, my love," returned my father.

" 'What do you want me to do?' said Kate.

" 'Only to hold the candle for me,' I answered, restored to my seven senses at last; and, taking it from her, I led the way, and she followed, till we had passed through the kitchen and reached the cellar-stairs. These were steep and awkward, and she let me help her down."

"Now, Edward!" said my mother.

"Yes, yes, my love, I understand," returned my father.

"Up to this time your mother had asked no questions; but when we stood in a vast, low cellar, which we had made several turns to reach, and I gave her the candle, and took up a great crowbar which lay on the floor, she said at last—

" 'Edward, are you going to bury me alive? or what *are* you going to do?'

" 'I'm going to dig you out,' I said, for I was nearly

*She looked so beautiful that I stood
staring at her without moving.*

beside myself with joy, as I struck the crowbar like a battering-ram into the wall. You can fancy, John, that I didn't work the worse that Kate was holding the candle for me.

"Very soon, though with great effort, I had dislodged a brick, and the next blow I gave into the hole sent back a dull echo. I was right!

"I worked now like a madman, and, in a very few minutes more, I had dislodged the whole of the brick-thick wall which filled up an archway of stone and curtained an ancient door in the lock of which the key now showed itself. It had been well greased, and I turned it without much difficulty.

"I took the candle from Kate, and led her into a spacious region of sawdust, cobweb, and wine-fungus.

" 'There, Kate!' I cried, in delight.

" 'But,' said Kate, 'will the wine be good?'

" 'General Fortescue will answer you that,' I returned, exultantly. 'Now come, and hold the light again while I find the port-bin.'

"I soon found not one, but several well-filled port-bins. Which to choose I could not tell. I must chance that. Kate carried a bottle and the candle, and I carried two bottles very carefully. We put them down in the kitchen with orders they should not be touched. We had soon carried the dozen to the hall-table by the dining-room door.

"When at length, with Jacob chuckling and rubbing his hands behind us, we entered the dining-room, Kate and I, for Kate would not part with her share in the joyful business, loaded with a level bottle in each hand, which we carefully erected on the sideboard, I presume, from the stare of the company, that we presented a rather remarkable appearance—Kate in her white muslin and I in my best clothes, covered with brick-dust, and cobwebs, and lime. But we could not be half so amusing to them as they were to us.

There they sat with the dessert before them but no wine-decanters forthcoming. How long they had sat thus, I have no idea. If you think your mamma has, you may ask her. Captain Calker and General Fortescue looked positively white about the gills. My uncle, clinging to the last hope, despairingly, had sat still and said nothing, and the guests could not understand the awful delay. Even Lady Georgiana had begun to fear a mutiny in the kitchen, or something equally awful. But to see the flash that passed across my uncle's face, when he saw us appear with *ported arms!* He immediately began to pretend that nothing had been the matter.

" 'What the deuce has kept you, Ned, my boy?' he said. 'Fair Hebe,' he went on, 'I beg your pardon. Jacob, you can go on decanting. It was very careless of you to forget it. Meantime, Hebe, bring that bottle to General Jupiter, there. He's got a corkscrew in the tail of his robe, or I'm mistaken.'

"Out came General Fortescue's corkscrew. I was trembling once more with anxiety. The cork gave the genuine plop; the bottle was lowered; glug, glug, glug, came from its beneficent throat, and out flowed something tawny as a lion's mane. The general lifted it lazily to his lips, saluting his nose on the way.

" 'Fifteen! by Gyeove!' he cried. 'Well, Admiral, this *was* worth waiting for! Take care how you decant that, Jacob—on peril of your life.'

"My uncle was triumphant. He winked hard at me not to tell. Kate and I retired, she to change her dress, I to get mine well brushed, and my hands washed. By the time I returned to the dining-room, no one had any questions to ask. For Kate, the ladies had gone to the drawing-room before she was ready, and I believe she had some difficulty in keeping my uncle's counsel. But she did.—Need I say that was the happiest Christmas I ever spent?"

"But how did you find the cellar, papa?" asked Effie.

"Where are your brains, Effie? Don't you remember I told you that I had a dream?"

"Yes. But you don't mean to say the existence of that wine-cellar was revealed to you in a dream?"

"But I do, indeed. I had seen the wine-cellar built up just before we left for Madeira. It was my father's plan for securing the wine when the house was let. And very well it turned out for the wine, and me too. I had forgotten all about it. Everything had conspired to bring it to my memory, but had just failed of success. I had fallen asleep under all the influences I told you of—influences from the region of my childhood. They operated still when I was asleep, and, all other distracting influences being removed, at length roused in my sleeping brain the memory of what I had seen. In the morning I remembered not my dream only, but the event of which my dream was a reproduction. Still, I was under considerable doubt about the place, and in this I followed the dream only, as near as I could judge.

"The admiral kept his word, and interposed no difficulties between Kate and me. Not that, to tell the truth, I was ever very anxious about that rock ahead; but it was very possible that his fastidious honour or pride might have occasioned a considerable interference with our happiness for a time. As it turned out, he could not leave me Culverwood, and I regretted the fact as little as he did himself. His gratitude to me was, however, excessive, assuming occasionally ludicrous outbursts of thankfulness. I do not believe he could have been more grateful if I had saved his ship and its whole crew. For his hospitality was at stake. Kind old man!"

Here ended my father's story, with a light sigh, a gaze into the bright coals, a kiss of my mother's hand which he held in his, and another glass of Burgundy.

PAPA'S STORY
A Scot's Christmas Story

O tell us a story, papa," said a wise-faced little girl, one winter night, as she intermitted for a moment her usual occupation of the hour before bedtime—that, namely, of sucking her thumb, earnestly and studiously followed, as if the fate of the world lay on the faithfulness of the process; "Do tell us a story, papa."

"Yes, do, papa," chimed in several more children. It is *such* a long time since you told us a story."

"I don't think papa ever told us a story," said one of the youngest.

"Oh, Dolly!" exclaimed half a dozen. But her next elder sister took up the speech.

"Yes, I dare say. But you were only born last year, and papa has been away for months and months."

Now, Dolly was five, and her papa had been away for three weeks.

"Well," interposed their papa, "I will try. What shall it be about?"

"Oh! about Scotland," cried the eldest.

"Why do you want a story about Scotland?"

"Because you will like it best yourself, papa."

"I don't want one about Scotland. I'm not a Scotchman, though papa is," cried Dolly, "I'm an Englishman."

Reprinted from *Illustrated London News* (1865).

"I like Scotch stories," said the sucker of thumbs; "only I can't understand the curious words. They sound so rough, I never can understand them."

"Well, my darlings, I will tell you one about Scotland, and there shan't be a Scotch word in it. If one single one comes out of my mouth you may punish me anyway you please."

"Oh, that's jolly! How shall we punish papa if he says one Scotch word?"

"Pull his beard!" said Dolly.

"No, that would be rude!" cried three or four.

Whereupon Dolly's face changed, and she took to her thumb, like Katy.

"Make him pay a fine."

"That's no use, papa's so rich!"

Whereas the chief difficulty papa had in telling the story was the thought of the butcher's bill popping in through twenty different keyholes.

"Make him pay a kiss to each of us for every word!"

"No, that would stop the story!"

"Kiss him to death when it's done!"

"Yes!—yes!—yes—kiss him to death when it's done!"

So it was agreed; and papa began.

"You know, my darlings, there are a great many hills in Scotland, which are green with grass to the very top, and the sheep feed all over them?"

"Oh, yes! I know! Like Hampstead-hill."

"No. Like that place in the City—Ludgate-hill."

"No, my dears; not like either of those. Just come to the window, and I will try to show you. You see that star shining so brightly away there?"

"Yes, But that is not a hill, papa; it's a star!"

"Yes, it's a star. But supoose you could not see that star for a great heap of rock and earth and stone rising up between you and the star, covered with grass, and with streams of water running down its sides in every direction, that heap would be a hill. And in some parts of Scotland there are a great many of these hills crowded together, only divided from each other by deep places called valleys. They all grow out of one root—that is the earth. The tops of these hills are high up and lonely in the air, with the stars above them, and often the clouds round about them like torn garments."

"What's *garments*, Kitty?"

"Frocks, Dolly."

"What tears them, then?"

"The wind tears them; and goes roaring and raving about the hills; and makes such a noise against the steep rocks, running into the holes in them and out again, that those hills are sometimes very awful places. But in the sunshine, although they do look lonely, they are so bright and beautiful, that all the boys and girls fancy the way to heaven lies up those hills."

"And doesn't it?"

"No."

"Where is it, then?"

"Ah! that's just what you come here to find out. But you must let me go on with my story now. In the winter, on the other hand, they are such wild howling places, with the hard hailstones beating upon them, and the soft, smothering snowflakes heaping up dreadful wastes of whiteness upon them, that if ever there was a child out on them he would die with fear, if he did not die with cold. But there are only sheep there, and they don't stay very high up the hills when the winter once begins to come over the mountains."

"What's mountains?"

"Mountains are higher hills yet."

"Higher yet! They can't be higher yet."

"Oh! yes, they are; and there are higher and higher

yet, till you could hardly believe it, even when you saw them.

"Well, as the winter comes over the tops of the hills the sheep come down their sides, because it is warmer the lower down you come; and even a foot thick of wool on their backs and sides could not keep out the terrible cold up there.

"But the sheep are not very knowing creatures, so they are something better instead. They are wise— that is, they are obedient—creatures, obedience being the very best wisdom. For, because they are not very knowing, they have a man to take care of them, who knows where to take them, especially when a storm comes on. Not that the sheep are so very silly as not to know where to go to get out of the wind, but they don't and can't think that some ways of getting out of danger are more dangerous still. They would lie down in a quiet place, and lie there till the snow settled down over them and smothered them. They would not feel it cold, their wool is so thick. Or they would tumble down steep places and be killed, or buried in the snow, or carried away by the stream at the bottom. So, though they know a little, they don't know enough, and need a shepherd to take care of them.

"Now the shepherd, though he is wise, is not quite clever enough for all that is wanted of him up in those strange, terrible hills; and he needs another to help him. Now, who do you think helps the shepherd? Ah! you know, Maggy; but you mustn't tell. I will tell. It is a curious creature with four legs—the shepherd has only two, you know;—and he is covered all over with long hair of three different colours mixed—black, and brown, and white; and he has a long nose and a longer tongue, which he knows how to hold. This tongue it is a great comfort to him sometimes to hang out of his mouth as far as ever it will hang. And he has a still longer tail, which is a greater comfort to him yet. I don't know what ever he would do without his tail; for, when his master speaks kindly to him, he is so full of delight, that I think he would die if he hadn't his tail to wag. He lets his gladness off by wagging his tail, so that it shan't burst his dear, honest, good dog-heart. Ah! there, I've told you. He's a dog, you see; and the very wisest and cleverest of all dogs. He could be taught anything. Only he is such a gentleman, though dressed very plainly, as a great many gentlemen are, that it would be a shame to teach him some of the things they teach commonplace rich dogs.

"Well, the shepherd tells the dog what he wants done, and off the dog runs to do it; for he can run three times as fast as the shepherd, and can get up and down places much better. I am not sure that he can see better than the shepherd, but I know he can smell better. So that he is just four legs and a long nose to the shepherd, besides the love he gives him which would comfort any good man, even if it were offered him by a hedgehog or a hen. And for his understanding, if I were to tell Willie how much I believe he understands—if I weren't his papa, that is—Willie, there, who has such a high opinion of his own judgment, and shakes his head so knowingly when he hears anything for the first time, as if it were a shame for anything to come into existence without letting him know first—Willie, I say, would consider me silly for believing it, or, what would be a great deal worse, would think that I didnt' really believe it, though I said it.

"One evening, in the beginning of April, the weakly sun of the season had gone down with a pale face behind the shoulder of a hill in the background of my story. If you had been there and had climbed up that hill, you would have seen him a great while longer, provided he had not, in the mean time, set behind a mountain of cloud, which, at this season of the year, he was very ready to do, and which, I suspect, he actually did this very evening about which I am telling you. And because he was gone down, the peat-fires upon the hearths of the cottages all began to glow more brightly, as if they were glad he was gone at last and had left them their work to do—or, rather, as if they wanted to do all they could to make up for his absence. And on one hearth in particular the peat-fire glowed very brightly. There was a pot hanging over it, with supper in it; and there was a little girl sitting by it, with a sweet, thoughtful face. Her hair was done up in a silken net, for it was the custom with Scotch girls—they wore no bonnet—to have their hair so arranged, many years before it became a fashion in London. She had a bunch of feathers, not in her hair, but fastened to her side by her apron-string, in the quill-ends of which was stuck the end of one of her knitting-needles, while the other was loose in her hand. But both were fast and busy in the loops of a blue-ribbed stocking, which she was knitting for her father.

"He was out on the hills. He had that morning taken his sheep higher up than before, and Nelly knew this; but it could not be long now till she would hear his footsteps, and measure the long stride between which brought him and happiness together."

"But hadn't she any mother?"

"Oh! yes, she had. If you had been in the cottage that night you would have heard a cough every now and then, and would have found that Nelly's mother was lying in a bed in the room—not a bed with curtains, but a bed with doors like a press. This does not seem a nice way of having a bed; but we should all be glad of the wooden curtain about us at night if we lived in such a cottage, on the side of a hill along which the wind swept like a wild river, only ten times faster than any river would run even down the hill-side. Through the cottage it would be spouting, and streaming, and eddying, and fighting, all night long; and a poor woman with a cough, or a man who has been out in the cold all day, is very glad of such a place to lie in, and leave the rest of the house to the wind and the fairies.

"Nelly's mother was ill, and there was little hope of her getting well again. What she could have done without Nelly, I can't think. It was so much easier to be ill with Nelly sitting there. For she was a good Nelly.

"After a while Nelly rose and put some peats on the fire, and hung the pot a link or two higher on the chain; for she was a wise creature, though she was only twelve, and could cook very well, because she took trouble, and thought about it. Then she sat down to her knitting again, which was a very frugal amusement.

" 'I wonder what's keeping your father, Nelly,' said her mother from the bed.

" 'I don't know, mother. It's not very late yet. He'll be home by and by. You know he was going over the shoulder of the hill to-day.'

"Now that was the same shoulder of the hill that the sun went down behind. And at the moment the sun was going down behind it, Nelly's father was standing on the top of it, and Nelly was looking up to the very place where he stood, and yet she did not see him. He was not too far off to be seen, but the sun was in her eyes, and the light of the sun hid him from her. He was then coming across with the sheep, to leave them for the night in a sheltered place—within a circle of stones that would keep the wind off them; and he ought, by rights, to have been home at least half an hour ago.—At length Nelly heard the distant

sound of a heavy shoe upon the point of a great rock
that grew up from the depths of the earth and just
came through the surface in the path leading across
the furze and brake to their cottage. She always
watched for that sound—the sound of her father's
shoe, studded thick with broad-headed nails, upon
the top of that rock. She started up; but instead of
rushing out to meet him, went to the fire and lowered
the pot. Then taking up a wooden bowl, half full of
oatmeal neatly pressed down into it, with a little salt
on the top, she proceeded to make a certain dish for
her father's supper, of which strong Scotchmen are
very fond. By the time her father reached the door,
it was ready, and set down with a plate over it to keep
it hot, though it had a great deal more need, I think,
to be let cool a little.

"When he entered, he looked troubled. He was a
tall man, dressed in rough grey cloth, with a broad,
round, blue bonnet, as they call it. His face looked
as if it had been weather-beaten into peace."

"Beaten into pieces, papa! How dreadful!"

"Be quiet, Dolly; that's not what papa means."

"I want to know, then."

"Well, Dolly, I think it would take twenty years at
least to make it plain to you, so I had better go on
with my story, especially as you will come to understand it one day without my explaining it. The shepherd's face, I say, was weatherbeaten and quiet, with
large, grand features, in which the docility of his dogs
and the gentleness of his sheep were mingled with
the strength and wisdom of a man who had to care
for both dogs and sheep.

" 'Well, Nelly,' he said, laying his hand on her forehead as she looked up into his face, 'how's your
mother?'

"And without waiting for an answer he went to the
bed, where the pale face of his wife lay upon the pil-

'Well, Nelly,' he said, laying his hand
on her forehead as she looked up into his face,
'how's your mother?'

low. She held out her thin, white hand to him, and he took it so gently in his strong, brown hand. But, before he had spoken, she saw the trouble on his face, and said,

" 'What has made you so late to-night, John?'

" 'I was nearly at the fold,' said the shepherd, 'before I saw that one of the lambs was missing. So, after I got them all in, I went back with the dogs to look for him.'

" 'Where's Jumper, then?' asked Nelly, who had been patting the neck and stroking the ears of the one dog which had followed at the shepherd's heels, and was now lying before the fire, enjoying the warmth none the less that he had braved the cold all day without minding it a bit.

" 'When we couldn't see anything of the lamb,' replied her father, 'I told Jumper to go after him and bring him to the house; and Blackfoot and I came home together. I doubt he'll have a job of it, poor dog! for it's going to be a rough night; but if dog can bring him, he will.'

"As the shepherd stopped speaking he seated himself by the fire and drew the wooden bowl towards him. Then he lifted his blue bonnet from his head, and said grace, half aloud, half murmured to himself. Then he put his bonnet on his head again, for his head was rather bald, and, as I told you, the cottage was a draughty place. And just as he put it on, a blast of wind struck the cottage and roared in the wide chimney. The next moment the rain dashed against the little window of four panes, and fell hissing into the peat-fire.

" 'There it comes,' said the shepherd.

" 'Poor Jumper!' said Nelly.

" 'And poor little lamb!' said the shepherd.

" 'It's the lamb's own fault,' said Nelly; 'he shouldn't have run away.'

" 'Ah! yes,' returned her father; 'but then the lamb didn't know what he was about exactly.'

"When the shepherd had finished his supper, he rose and went out to see whether Jumper and the lamb were coming; but the dark night would have made the blackest dog and the whitest lamb both of one colour, and he soon came in again. Then he took the Bible and read a chapter to his wife and daughter, which did them all good, even though Nelly did not understand very much of it. And then he prayed a prayer, and was very near praying for Jumper and the lamb, only he could not quite. And there he was wrong. He should have prayed about whatever troubled him or could be done good to. But he was such a good man that I am almost ashamed of saying he was wrong.

"And just as he came to the *Amen* in his prayer, there came a whine to the door. And he rose from his knees and went and opened the door. And there was the lamb with Jumper behind him. And Jumper looked dreadfully wet, and draggled, and tired, and the curls had all come out of his long hair. And yet he seemed as happy as a dog could be, and looked up in the face of the shepherd triumphantly, as much as to say, 'Here he is, Master!' And the lamb looked scarcely anything the worse; for his thick, oily wool had kept away the wet; and he hadn't been running about everywhere looking for Jumper as Jumper had been for him.

"And Jumper, after Nelly had given him his supper, lay down by the fire beside the other dog, which made room for him to go next to the glowing peats; and the lamb, which had been eating all day and didn't want any supper, lay down beside him. And then Nelly bade her father and mother and the dogs good-night, and went away to bed likewise, thinking the wind might blow as it pleased now, for sheep and dogs, and father and all, were safe for the whole of the dark, windy hours between that and the morning. It is so nice to know that there is a long *nothing to do;*—but only after everything is done.

"But there are other winds in the world besides those which shake the fleeces of sheep and the beards of men, or blow ships to the bottom of the sea, or scatter the walls of cottages abroad over the hillsides. There are winds that blow up huge storms inside the hearts of men and women, and blow till the great clouds full of tears go up, and rain down from the eyes to quiet them.

"What can papa mean?"

"Never you mind, Dolly. You'll know soon enough. I'm fourteen, and I know what papa means."

"Nelly lay down in her warm bed, feeling as safe and snug as ever child felt in a large, rich house in a great city. For there was the wind howling outside to make it all the quieter inside; and there was the great, bare, cold hill before the window, which, although she could not see it, and only knew that it was there, made the bed in which she lay so close, and woolly, and warm. Now this bed was separated from her father and mother's only by a thin partition, and she heard them talking. And they had not talked long before that other cold wind that was blowing through their hearts blew into hers too. And I will tell you what they said to each other that made the cold wind blow into her heart.

" 'It wasn't the loss of the lamb, John, that made you look so troubled when you came home to-night,' said her mother.

" 'No, it wasn't, Jane, I must confess,' returned her father.

" 'You've heard something about Harry.'

" 'I can't deny it.'

" 'What is it?'

" 'I'll tell you in the morning.'

" 'I shan't sleep a wink for thinking whatever it can be, John. You had better tell me now. If the Lord would only bring that stray lamb back to his fold, I should die happy—sorry as I should be to leave Nelly and you, my own John.'

" 'Don't talk about dying, Nelly. It breaks my heart.'

" 'We won't talk about it, then. But what's this about Harry? And how came you to hear it?'

" 'I was close to the hill-road, when I saw James Jamieson, the carrier, coming up the hill with his cart. I ran and met him.'

" 'And he told you? What did he tell you?'

" 'Nothing very particular. He only hinted that he had heard, from Wauchope the merchant, that a certain honest man's son—he meant me, Nelly—was going the wrong road. And I said to James Jamieson—What road could the man mean? And James said to me—He meant the broad road, of course. And I sat down on a stone, and I heard no more; at least, I could not make sense of what James went on to say; and when I lifted my head, James and his cart were just out of sight over the top of the hill. I daresay that was how I lost the lamb.'

"A deep silence followed, and Nelly understood that her mother could not speak. At length a sob and a low weeping came through the boards to her keen mountain ear. But not another word was spoken; and, although Nelly's heart was sad, she soon fell fast asleep.

"Now, Willie had gone to college, and had been a very good boy for the first winter. They go to college only in winter in Scotland. And he had come home in the end of March and had helped his father to work their little farm, doing his duty well to the sheep and to everything and everybody; for learning had not made him the least unfit for work. Indeed, work that learning does really make a man unfit for, cannot be fit work for that man—perhaps is not fit work for anybody. When winter came, he had gone back to Edinburgh, and he ought to have been home a week ago, and he had not come. He had written to say that he had to finish some lessons he had begun to give, and could not be home till the end of the month. Now this was so far true that it was not a lie. But there was more in it: he did not want to go home to the lonely hillside—so lonely, that there were only a father and a mother and a sister there. He had made acquaintance with some students who were fonder of drinking whisky than of getting up in the morning to write abstracts, and he didn't want to leave them.

"Annie was, as I have said, too young to keep awake because she was troubled; and so, before half an hour was over, was fast asleep and dreaming. And the wind outside, tearing at the thatch of the cottage, mingled with her dream.

"I will tell you what her dream was.—She thought they were out in the dark and the storm, she and her father. But she was no longer Nelly; she was Jumper. And her father said to her, 'Jumper, go after the black lamb and bring him home.' And away she galloped over the stones, and through the furze, and across the streams, and up the rocks, and jumped the stone fences, and swam the pools of water, to find the little black lamb. And all the time, somehow or other, the little black lamb was her brother Willie. And nothing could turn the dog Jumper, though the wind blew as if it would blow him off all his four legs, and off the hill, as one blows a fly off a book. And the hail beat in Jumper's face, as if it would put out his eyes or knock holes in his forehead, and yet Jumper went on."

"But it wasn't Jumper; it was Nelly, you know."

"I know that, but I am talking about the dog

Jumper, that Nelly thought she was. He went on and on, and over the top of the cold, wet hill, and was beginning to grow hopeless about finding the black lamb, when, just a little way down the other side, he came upon him behind a rock. He was standing in a miry pool, all wet with rain. Jumper would never have found him, the night was so dark and the lamb was so black, but that he gave a bleat; whereupon Jumper tried to say 'Willie', but could not, and only gave a gobbling kind of bark. So he jumped upon the lamb, and taking a mouthful of his wool, gave him a shake that made him pull his feet out of the mire, and then drove him off before him, trotting all the way home. When they came into the cottage, the black lamb ran up to Nelly's mother, and jumped into her bed, and Jumper jumped in after him; and then Nelly was Nelly and Willie was Willie, as they used to be, when Nelly would creep into Willie's bed in the morning and kiss him awake. Then Nelly woke, and was sorry that it was a dream. For Willie was still away, far off on the broad road, and how ever was he to be got home? Poor black lamb!

"She soon made up her mind. Only how to carry out her mind was the difficulty. All day long she thought about it. And she wrote a letter to her father, telling him what she was going to do; and when she went to her room the next night, she laid the letter on her bed, and, putting on her Sunday bonnet and cloak, waited till they should be asleep.

"The shepherd had gone to bed very sad. He, too, had been writing a letter. It had taken him all the evening to write, and Nelly had watched his face while he wrote it, and seen how the muscles of it worked with sorrow and pain as he slowly put word after word down on the paper. When he had finished it, and folded it up, and put a wafer on it, and addressed it, he left it on the table, and, as I said, went to bed, where he soon fell asleep; for even sorrow does not often keep people awake that have worked hard through the day in the open air. And Nelly was watching.

"When she thought he was asleep, she took a pair of stockings out of a chest and put them in her pocket. Then, taking her Sunday shoes in her hand, she stepped gently from her room to the cottage door, which she opened easily, for it was never locked. She then found that it was pitch dark; but she could keep the path well enough, for her bare feet told her at once when she was going off it. It is a great blessing to have bare feet. People with bare feet can always keep the path better, and keep their garments cleaner, too. Only they must be careful to wash them at night.

"So, dark as it was, she soon reached the road. There was no wind that night, and the clouds hid the stars. She would turn in the direction of Edinburgh, and let the carrier overtake her. For she felt rather guilty, and was anxious to get on.

"After she had walked a good while, she began to wonder that the carrier had not come up with her. The fact was that the carrier never left till the early morning. She was not a bit afraid, though, reasoning that, as she was walking in the same direction, it would take him so much the longer to get up with her.

"At length, after walking a long way—longer far than she thought, for she walked a great part of it half asleep—she began to feel a little tired, and sat down upon a stone by the roadside. There was a stone behind her, too. She could just see its grey face. She leaned her back against it, and fell fast asleep.

"When she woke she could not think where she was, or how she had got there. It was a dark, drizzly morning, and her feet were cold. But she was quite dry. For the rock against which she fell asleep in the night projected so far over her head that it had kept all the rain off her. She could not have chosen a better place, if she had been able to choose. But the sight around her was very dreary. In front lay a swampy ground, creeping away, dismal and wretched, to the horizon, where a long low hill closed it. Behind her rose a mountain, bare and rocky, on which neither sheep nor shepherd was to be seen. Her home seemed to have vanished in the night, and left her either in a dream or in another world. And as she came to herself, the fear grew upon her that either she had missed the way in the dark or the carrier had gone past while she slept, either of which was dreadful to contemplate. She began to feel hungry, too, and she had not had the foresight to bring even a piece of oatcake with her.

"It was only dusky dawn yet. There was plenty of time. She would sit down again for a little while; for the rock had a homely look to her. It had been her refuge all night, and she was not willing to leave it. So she leaned her arms on her knees, and gazed out upon the dreary, grey, misty flat before her.

"Then she rose, and, turning her back on the waste, kneeled down, and prayed God that, as he taught Jumper to find lambs, he would teach her to find her brother. And thus she fell fast asleep again.

"When she woke once more and turned towards the road, whom should she see standing there but the carrier, staring at her. And his big strong horses stood in the road too, with their carts behind them. They were not in the least surprised. She could not help crying, just a little, for joy.

" 'Why, Nelly, what on earth are you doing here?' said the carrier.

" 'Waiting for you,' answered Nelly.

" 'Where are you going, child?'

" 'To Edinburgh.'

" 'What on earth are you going to do in Edinburgh?'

" 'I am going to my brother Willie, at the college.'

" 'But the college is over now.'

" 'I know that,' said Nelly.

" 'What's his address, then?' the carrier went on.

" 'I don't know,' answered Nelly.

" 'It's a lucky thing that I know, then. But you have no business to leave home this way.'

" 'Oh! yes, I have.'

" 'I am sure your father did not know of it, for when he gave me a letter this morning to take to Willie he did not say a word about you.'

" 'He thought I was asleep in my bed,' returned Nelly, trying to smile. But the thought that the carrier had actually seen her father since she left home, was too much for her, and she cried.

" 'I can't go back with you now,' said the carrier, 'so you must go on with me.'

" 'That's just what I want,' said Nelly.

"So the carrier made her put on her shoes and stockings, for he was a kind man and had children of his own. Then he pulled out some of the straw that packed his cart, and made her a little bed on the tarpaulin that covered it, just where there was a soft bundle beneath. Then he lifted her up on it and covered her over with a few empty sacks. There Nelly was so happy, and warm, and comfortable, that, for the third time, she fell asleep.

"When she woke he gave her some bread and cheese for her breakfast, and some water out of a brook that crossed the road, and then Nelly began to look about her. The rain had ceased and the sun was shining, and the country looked very pleasant; but Nelly thought it a strange country. She could see so much farther! And corn was growing everywhere, and there was not a sheep to be seen, and there were many cows feeding in the fields.

161

" 'Are we near Edinburgh?' she asked.

" 'Oh, no!' answered the carrier; 'we are a long way from Edinburgh yet.'

"And so they journeyed on. The day was flecked all over with sunshine and rain; and when the rain's turn came, Nelly would creep under a corner of the tarpaulin till it was over. They slept part of the night at a small town they passed through.

"Nelly thought it a very long way to Edinburgh, though the carrier was kind to her, and gave her of everything that he had himself, except the whisky, which he did not think good for her.

"At length she spied, far away, a great hill, that looked like a couching lion.

" 'Do you see that hill?' said the carrier.

" 'I am just looking at it,' answered Nelly.

" 'Edinburgh lies at the foot of that hill.'

" 'Oh!' said Nelly; and scarcely took her eyes off it till it went out of sight again.

"Reaching the brow of an eminence, they saw Arthur's Seat (as the carrier said the hill was called) once more, and below it a great jagged ridge of what Nelly took to be broken rocks. But the carrier told her that was the Old Town of Edinburgh. Those fierce-looking splinters on the edge of the mass were the roofs, gables, and chimneys of the great houses once inhabited by the nobility of Scotland. But when you come near the houses you find them shabby-looking; for they are full of poor people, who cannot keep them clean and nice.

"But, certainly, my children, if you will excuse your Scotch papa for praising his own country's capital, I don't believe there ever was a city that looked so grand from the distance as that Old Town of Edinburgh. And when you get into the streets you can fancy yourself hundreds of years back in the story of Scotland. Seen thus through the perspective of time or distance, it is a great marvel to everyone with any imagination at all; and it was nothing less to little Nelly, even when she got into the middle of it. But her heart was so full of its dog-duties towards her black lamb of a brother that the toyshops and the sugar-plum-shops could not draw it towards their mines of wonder and wealth.

"At length the cart stopped at a public-house in the Grassmarket—a wide, open place, with strange old houses all round it, and a huge rock, with a castle on its top, towering over it. There Nelly got down.

" 'I can't go with you till I've unloaded my cart,' said the carrier.

" 'I don't want you to go with me, please,' said Nelly. 'I think Willie would rather not. Please give me father's letter.'

"So the carrier gave her the letter, and got a little boy of the landlady's to show her the way up the West-bow—a street of tall houses, so narrow that you might have shaken hands across it from window to window. But those houses are all pulled down now, I am sorry to say, and the street Nelly went up has vanished. From the West-bow they went up a stair into the High-street, and thence into a narrow court, and then up a winding stair, and so came to the floor where Willie's lodging was. There the little boy left Nelly.

"Nelly knocked two or three times before anybody came; and when at last a woman opened the door, what do you think the woman did the moment she inquired after Willie?—She shut the door in her face with a fierce, scolding word. For Willie had vexed her that morning, and she thoughtlessly took her revenge upon Nelly without even asking her a question. Then, indeed, for a moment, Nelly's courage gave way. All at once she felt dreadfully tired, and sat down upon the stair and cried. And the landlady was so angry with Willie that she forgot all about the little girl that wanted to see him.

"So for a whole hour Nelly sat upon the stair, moving only to let people pass. She felt dreadfully miserable, but had not the courage to knock again, for fear of having the door shut in her face yet more hopelessly. At last a woman came up and knocked at the door. Nelly rose trembling and stood behind her. The door opened; the woman was welcomed; she entered. The door was again closing when Nelly cried out in agony,

" 'Please, ma'am, I want to see my brother Willie!' and burst into sobs.

"The landlady, her wrath having by this time assuaged, was vexed with herself and ashamed that she had not let the child in.

" 'Bless me!' she cried; 'have you been there all this time? Why didn't you tell me you were Willie's sister? Come in. You won't find him in, though. It's not much of his company we get, I can tell you.'

" 'I don't want to come in, then,' sobbed Nelly. 'Please to tell me where he is, ma'am.'

" 'How should I know where he is? At no good, I warrant. But you had better come in and wait, for it's your only chance of seeing him before to-morrow morning.'

"With a sore heart Nelly went in and sat down by the kitchen fire. And the landlady and her visitor sat and talked together, every now and then casting a look at Nelly, who kept her eyes on the ground, waiting with all her soul till Willie should come. Every time the landlady looked, she looked sooner the next time; and every time she looked, Nelly's sad face went deeper into her heart; so that, before she knew what was going on in herself, she quite loved the child; for she was a kind-hearted woman, though she was sometimes cross.

"In a few minutes she went up to Nelly and took her bonnet off. Nelly submitted without a word. Then she made her a cup of tea; and while Nelly was taking it she asked her a great many questions. Nelly answered them all; and the landlady stared with amazement at the child's courage and resolution, and thought with herself.

" 'Well, if anything can get Willie out of his bad ways, this little darling will do it.'

"Then she made her go to Willie's bed, promising to let her know the moment he came home.

"Nelly slept and slept till it was night. When she woke it was dark, but a light was shining through beneath the door. So she rose and put on her frock and shoes and stockings, and went to the kitchen.

" 'You see he's not come yet, Nelly,' said the landlady.

" 'Where can he be?' returned Nelly, sadly.

" 'Oh! he'll be drinking with some of his companions in the public-house, I suppose.'

" 'Where is the public-house?'

" 'There are hundreds of them, child.'

" 'I know the place he generally goes to,' said a young tradesman who sat by the fire.

"He had a garret-room in the house, and knew Willie by sight. And he told the landlady in a low voice where it was.

" 'Oh! do tell me, please sire,' cried Nelly. 'I want to get him home.'

" 'You don't think he'll mind you, do you?'

" 'Yes, I do,' returned Nelly confidently.

" 'Well, I'll show you the way if you like; but you'll find it a rough place, I can tell you. You'll wish yourself out of it pretty soon, with or without Willie.'

" 'I won't leave it without him,' said Nelly, tying on her bonnet.

" 'Stop a bit,' said the landlady. 'You don't think I

am going to let the child out with nobody but you to look after her?"

" 'Come along, then, ma'am.'

"The landlady put on her bonnet, and out they all went into the street.

"What a wonder it *might* have been to Nelly! But she only knew that she was in the midst of great lights, and carts and carriages rumbling over the stones, and windows full of pretty things, and crowds of people jostling along the pavements. In all the show she wanted nothing but Willie.

"The young man led them down a long dark close through an archway, and then into a court off the close, and then up an outside stone stair to a low-browed door, at which he knocked.

" 'I don't much like the look of this place,' said the landlady.

" 'Oh! there's no danger, I dare say, if you keep quiet. They never hurt the child. Besides, her brother'll see to that.'

"Presently the door was opened, and the young man asked after Willie.

" 'Is he in?' he said.

" 'He may be, or he may not,' answered a fat, frouzy woman, in a dirty cotton dress. 'Who wants him?'

" 'This little girl.'

" 'Please ma'am, I'm his sister.'

" 'We want no sisters here.'

"And she proceeded to close the door. I dare say the landlady remembered with shame that that was just what she had done that morning.

" 'Come! come!' interposed the young tradesman, putting his foot between the door and the post; 'don't be foolish. Surely you won't go to keep a child like that from speaking to her own brother! Why, the Queen herself would let her in.'

"This softened the woman a little, and she hesitated, with the latch in her hand.

" 'Mother wants him,' said Nelly. 'She's very ill. I heard her cry about Willie. Let me in.'

"She took hold of the woman's hand, who drew it away hastily, but stepped back, at the same time, and let her enter. She then resumed her place at the door.

" 'Devil a one of *you* shall come in!' she said, as if justifying the child's admission by the exclusion of the others.

" 'We don't want, mistress,' said the young man. 'But we'll just see that no harm comes to her.'

" 'D'ye think I'm not enough for that?' said the woman, with scorn. 'Let me see who dares to touch her! But you may stay where you are, if you like. The air's free.'

"So saying, she closed the door, with a taunting laugh.

"The passage was dark in which Nelly found herself; but she saw a light at the further end, through a keyhole, and heard the sounds of loud talk and louder laughter. Before the woman had closed the outer door, she had reached this room; nor did the woman follow either to guide or prevent her.

"A pause came in the noise. She tapped at the door.

" 'Come in!' cried someone. And she entered.

"Round a table were seated four youths, drinking. Of them one was Willie, with flushed face and flashing eyes. They all stared when the child stood before them, in her odd, old-fashioned bonnet, and her little shawl pinned at the throat. Willie stared as much as any of them.

"Nelly spoke first.

" 'Willie! Willie!' she cried, and would have rushed to him, but the table was between.

167

" 'What do you want here, Nelly? Who the deuce let you come here?' said Willie, not quite unkindly.

" 'I want you, Willie. Come home with me. Oh! please come home with me.'

" 'I can't, now, Nelly, you see,' he answered. Then, turning to his companions, 'How could the child have found her way here?' he said, looking ashamed as he spoke.

" 'You're fetched. That's all,' said one of them, with a sneer. 'Mother's sent for you.'

" 'Go along!' said another; 'and mind you don't catch it when you get home!'

" 'Nobody will say a word to you, Willie,' interposed Nelly.

" 'Be a good boy, and don't do it again!' said the third, raising his glass to his lips.

"Willie tried to laugh, but was evidently vexed.

" 'What are you standing there for, Nelly?' he said, sharply. 'This is no place for you.'

" 'Nor for you either, Willie,' returned Nelly, without moving.

" 'We're all very naughty, aren't we, Nelly?' said the first.

" 'Come and give me a kiss, and I'll forgive you,' said the second.

" 'You shan't have your brother; so you may trudge home again without him,' said the third.

"And then they all burst out laughing, except Willie.

" 'Do go away, Nelly,' he said, angrily.

" 'Where am I to go to?' she asked.

" 'Where you came from.'

" 'That's home,' said Nelly; 'but I can't go home to-night, and I daren't go home without you. Mother would die. She's very ill, Willie. I heard her crying last night.'

"It seemed to Nelly at the moment that it was only last night she left home.

"I'll just take the little fool to my lodgings and come back directly,' said Willie, rather stricken at this mention of his mother.

" 'Oh! yes. Do as you're bid!' they cried, and burst out laughing again. For they despised Willie because he was only a shepherd's son, although they liked to have his company because he was clever. But Willie was angry now.

" 'I tell you what,' he said, 'I'll go when and where I like.'

Two of them were silent now, because they were afraid of Willie; for he was big and strong. The third, however, trusting to the others, said, with a nasty sneer,

" 'Go with its little sister to its little mammy!'

"Now Willie could not get out, so small was the room and so large the table, except one or other of those next him rose to let him pass. Neither did. Willie therefore jumped on the table, kicked the tumbler of the one who had last spoken into the breast of his shirt, jumped down, took Nelly by the hand, and left the house.

" 'The rude boys!' said Nelly. 'I would never go near them again, if I was you, Willie.'

"But Willie said never a word, for he was not pleased with Nelly, or with himself, or with his *friends*.

"When they got into the house he said, abruptly, 'What's the matter with mother, Nelly?'

" 'I don't know, Willie; but I don't think she'll ever get better. I'm sure father doesn't think it either.'

"Willie was silent for a long time. Then he said,

" 'How did you come here, Nelly?'

"And Nelly told him the whole story.

" 'And now you'll come home with me, Willie.'

" 'It was very foolish of you, Nelly. To think you could bring me home if I didn't choose!'

" 'But you do choose, don't you, Willie?'

" 'You might as well have written,' he said.

"Then Nelly remembered her father's letter, which the carrier had given her. And Willie took it, and sat down, with his back to Nelly, and read it through. Then he burst out crying, and laid his head on his arms and went on crying. And Nelly got upon a bar of the chair—for he was down on the table—and leaned over him, and put her arms round his neck, and said, crying herself all the time,

" 'Nobody said a word to the black lamb when Jumper brought him home, Willie.'

"And Willie lifted his head, and put his arms round Nelly, and drew her face to his, and kissed her as he used to kiss her years ago.

"And I needn't tell you anything more about it."

"Oh! yes. Tell us how they got home."

"They went home with the carrier the next day."

"And wasn't his father glad to see Willie?"

"He didn't say much. He held out his hand with a half smile on his mouth, and a look in his eye like the moon before a storm."

"And his mother?"

"His mother held out her arms, and drew him down to her bosom, and stroked his hair, and prayed God to bless Willie, her boy."

"And Nelly—weren't they glad to see Nelly?"

"They made more of Willie than they did of Nelly."

"And wasn't Nelly sorry?"

"No; she never noticed it—she was so busy making much of Willie, too."

"But I hope they didn't scold Nelly for going to fetch Willie?"

"When she went to bed that night, her father kissed her and said,

" 'The blessin' o' an auld father be upo' ye, my wee bairn!'

"There's Scotch," now exclaimed the whole company.

And in one moment papa was on the floor, buried beneath a mass of children.

The chief thumbsucker, after kissing till she was stupid, recovered her wits by sucking her thumb diligently for a whole minute, after which she said, "If we had been wolves, it would have been dangerous, papa."

And then they all went to bed.

CORAGE, GOD MEND AL